The Dark Room

R. K. NARAYAN

The Dark Room

The University of Chicago Press
Chicago and London
in association with
William Heinemann, Ltd.

The University of Chicago Press, Chicago 60637
The University of Chicago Press, Ltd., London
William Heinemann, Ltd., 10 Upper Grosvenor Street, London
All rights reserved. Published 1938
This edition 1981

Printed in the United States of America

85 84 83 82 81   5 4 3 2 1

Library of Congress Cataloging in Publication Data

Narayan, R. K. 1906–
  The dark room.

  I. Title.
PR9499.3.N3D37 1981   823   80-39930
ISBN 0-226-56836-9
ISBN 0-226-56837-7 (pbk.)

Chapter One

AT schooltime Babu suddenly felt very ill, and Savitri fussed over him and put him to bed. And in bed he stayed till Ramani came in and asked, " What is this ? "

" Nothing," said Savitri, and passed into the kitchen. Ramani questioned the patient himself and called " Savitri ! " Before she could answer, he called her twice again, and asked, " Are you deaf ? "

" I was just——"

" What is the matter with Babu ? "

" He is not well."

" You are too ready with your medical certificate. Babu, get up ! Don't miss your school on any account."

Babu turned on his mother a look of appeal. She said, " Lie down, Babu. You are not going to school today."

Ramani said, " Mind your own business, do you hear ? "

" The boy has fever."

" No, he hasn't. Go and do any work you like in the kitchen, but leave the training of a grown-up boy to me. It is none of a woman's business."

I

" Can't you see how ill the boy is ? "

" All right, all right," Ramani said contemptuously. " It is getting late for my office." He went to the dining-room.

Babu dressed and slunk off to school. Savitri gave him a tumbler of milk and saw him off. She returned to the kitchen. Her husband had already begun his meal, served by the cook.

She asked again, " Can't you see how ill the boy is ? "

Ramani did not deign to hear the question, but asked, " Who selected the vegetables for this meal ? "

" Why ? "

" Brinjals, cucumber, radish, and greens, all the twelve months in the year and all the thirty days in the month. I don't know when I shall have a little decent food to eat. I slave all day in the office for this mouthful. No lack of expenses, money for this and money for that. If the cook can't cook properly, do the work yourself. What have you to do better than that ? "

Savitri hovered between the cook and her husband, watching every item on his dining-leaf, and instructing the cook to bring a second or a third helping. This was by no means an easy task, for Ramani was eccentric and lawless in his taste. " Why do you torment me with this cucumber for the dozenth time? Do you think I live on it?" Or he would say, if there was the slightest delay, " Ah, ah! I suppose I'll have to apply to my office for leave and wait for this salted cucumber! A fine thing. Never knew people could be so niggardly with cucumber, the cheapest trash in the market. Why not have cut up a few more, instead of trying to feed the whole household on a quarter of it? Fine economy. Wish you'd show the same economy in other matters." Savitri never interrupted this running commentary with an explanation, and her silence sometimes infuriated her husband. " Saving up your energy by being silent! Saving it up for what purpose? When a man asks you something you could do worse than honour him with a reply." Sometimes, if she offered an explanation, as occasionally happened, she would be told, " Shut up. Words won't mend a piece of foul cooking."

After the meal he hurried away to his room and dressed for his office. This was an elaborate ritual, complicated by haste. Ramani would keep calling the servant Ranga in order to tell him what he was and where he ought to be for not polishing the boots properly, for folding the trousers with a wrong crease, for leaving the coat on the frame with all the pockets bulging out. Savitri, too, would sometimes be told what

3

her husband thought of her for not attending to buttons or sock-holes, and for not keeping an eye on Ranga. Every item of dress infuriated Ramani and incited him to comment, with the exception of ties, which received his personal attention. He kept them carefully pressed between the leaves of three bulky books which he had on his table : a heavy Annandale's Dictionary, a *Complete Works* of Byron, and an odd volume of the *Encyclopaedia Britannica* contained between them all his best ties.

Dressed in a silk suit, and with a sun-hat on, he stood at the street door and called, " Who is there ? " which meant, " Savitri, come here and see me off." When Savitri came he said, " Close this door."

" I have finished all the change. I shall have to buy some vegetables for the evening."

" Will a rupee do ? " He gave her the money and strode out. For a moment Savitri lingered in the doorway to hear the protests and growls of the old Chevrolet as it was taken out of the garage. When the noise of the engine ceased, a calm fell on the house.

Now Savitri had before her a little business with her god. She went to the worshipping-room, lighted the wicks and incense, threw on the images on the wooden pedestal handfuls of hibiscus, jasmine and nerium, and muttered all

4

the sacred chants she had learnt from her mother years ago. She prostrated herself before the god, rose, picked up a dining-leaf, and sat down in the kitchen. The cook served her with a doleful face. He asked, " Are the preparations very bad today, madam ? " He was very sensitive to criticism and every day he smarted while his master talked at dinner.

" We ought not to have repeated the brinjals today. We had it yesterday," Savitri said. "No more of it this week, whatever happens."

"All right, madam. Are the preparations very bad this morning ? "

" Not exactly bad. Perhaps you would have done well to reduce the tamarind in the sauce. Your master doesn't like tamarind very much."

The cook served her in sullen silence. Every day this happened. He was affected acutely both by criticism and by hunger, and criticism hurt him all the more because he lived in a state of protracted hunger, being the last to eat. Other cooks might have eased the situation by snatching a gulp of milk or curd when the mistress was not looking their way, but not he; Savitri locked up these commodities in the kitchen cupboard and served them out herself.

" I don't know ; master is never satisfied. I do my best, and what more can a human being do ? "

As this was almost a daily lament as regular as her husband's lecture, Savitri ceased to pay attention to it and ate in silence. Her thoughts reverted to Babu. The boy looked unwell, and perhaps at that moment was very ill in his class. How impotent she was, she thought; she had not the slightest power to do anything at home, and that after fifteen years of married life. Babu did look very ill and she was powerless to keep him in bed ; she felt she ought to have asserted herself a little more at the beginning of her married life and then all would have been well. There were girls nowadays who took charge of their husbands the moment they were married ; there was her own friend Gangu who had absolutely tethered up her poor man.

After food she went to her bench in the hall and lay down on it, chewing a little areca-nut and a few betel leaves, and browsed over the pages of a Tamil magazine. In half an hour the house became perfectly still. The servant had finished the day's washing and gone to a near-by shop for a smoke ; the cook was out for an hour in order to meet his friends at a coffee-house and compare kitchen politics. Odd noises of crows and sparrows in the garden broke the stillness of the hour. Over the pages of the magazine Savitri snatched a brief nap.

The clatter of the one o'clock bell from the

Extension Elementary School reached her drowsing mind and woke her up. It was the recess hour and her two daughters, Sumati and Kamala, would be here presently, jumping about in their haste. Savitri went to the kitchen to mix curd and rice for the girls. Just as she was opening the kitchen cupboard she heard footsteps in the hall and almost immediately Kamala, a plump little girl with a springy pigtail, burst into the kitchen and sat down with her plate before her. She was panting for breath.

" How often am I to tell you not to come running in the sun ? Where is Sumati ? "

" She is coming with her friends."

" Why couldn't you have come with her ? "

" She won't allow me in her company. They are all in the Eighth Class."

Kamala stuffed a few mouthfuls and tried to rise. Savitri pushed her down in her seat and said, "You have got to eat the whole of it. I mixed only a little." Kamala wriggled and protested.

" It is getting late, Mother. I must go. I can't go on eating all day."

" I will give you three pies. Finish it."

" All right," said Kamala, and related to her mother some of the day's events in the school. " Our teacher caned Sambu today. He is a bad

7

boy, Mother. He threw a big stone at another boy's toes. Every day he threatens to snatch away my notebooks."

Kamala had picked up her slate and books and was ready to start when her elder sister Sumati came in. "Are you going back to school already, Kamala ? " she asked authoritatively.

" Yes."

" Mother," Sumati cried, " why do you let Kamala go back so early ? We have still half an hour."

Savitri said, " Here, Kamala, what is the hurry ? "

" I have some work. I have to go," said Kamala, and vanished.

Sumati went to her desk, carefully put away her books of the morning, and took out her afternoon lessons ; she arranged her notebooks in a pile and placed on top the yellow cardboard box in which she kept a number of pencils, a rubber and some pieces of coloured thread. She was examining the points of her pencils when Savitri came to her desk and exclaimed, " So leisurely ! "

" Our music-teacher said he would come late today——"

" Your rice is ready."

At the mention of rice Sumati made a wry face. " I'm not hungry, Mother."

Savitri glared at her. " Don't annoy me, madam."

" I'm tired of eating rice, nothing but rice morning, noon, and night."

Sumati went to the kitchen and sat down before her plate. Savitri watched her as she ate and wondered why this girl was getting thinner every day. She was eleven years old and still looked as she did three years ago, as if a whiff of wind could push her off her feet, frail and floating. Perhaps nothing wrong in it ; must be hereditary, must be taking after her grand-mother : every feature, the dusky colour, the small mouth, rather small eyes, and straight hair. " As my mother must have looked about forty years ago."

" Mother, I shall want four annas on Monday," said Sumati.

" What for ? "

" I have to buy an embroidery pattern book."

" All right. By the way, why don't you keep Kamala with you and see that she doesn't come running through the streets ? "

" She doesn't listen to me, Mother."

" But she said you wouldn't allow her in your company."

" She is such a nuisance to my friends. She keeps asking everyone for pencils and ribbons. It is disgraceful."

" All the same, keep an eye on the girl."

After Sumati went back to school Savitri sat down for a moment fretting about the cook. It was two and he hadn't come yet. How often had she to tell him to be back before two o'clock ? He never returned before two-thirty and delayed coffee and tiffin till three-thirty— and close on its heels would come the planning of the night dinner, and on and on endlessly. Was there nothing else for one to do than attend to this miserable business of the stomach from morning till night ?

The cook walked in at about two-thirty. " I was about to light the oven for coffee," said Savitri.

" Why, madam ? Not at all necessary."

" If you can't be back at two o'clock, you can tell me. I will do this tiffin business myself. I do so many things already one more will make no difference. You can come at your leisure and do whatever is left undone."

The cook went to the kitchen in a rage, muttering, " One always comes back, one never goes out to be gone for ever. How is one to know whether it is two or two-thirty ? No two clocks agree. When the school bell went off at two o'clock, the clock in the hotel showed only one-forty-five. If you want me to be punctual, why can't you buy a watch for me ? " When

Savitri entered the kitchen a little later he told her, " From tomorrow I propose to stay here in the afternoon and not go out anywhere." Savitri said, " I've no objection to your going out, but if you don't come back at two o'clock this miserable business for the stomach will continue the whole day——" She issued a few instructions in regard to the night dinner and said, " I'm going out. If the children come from school before I return, give them coffee and tiffin. Babu will come in the evening. He is not quite well. Give him coffee. Don't compel him to take tiffin if he doesn't want it."

She dressed her hair, washed her face, renewed the vermilion mark on her forehead, looked at her *saree* for a moment, wondering whether she should wear another and dismissing the thought with, " This is quite good ; I'm not going outside the Extension." She was ready to go out on her afternoon round of visits at three-thirty. She called the cook and told him : " Tell the children I'll be back very soon. Don't forget about Babu's coffee."

§

At eight-thirty Savitri's ears, as ever, were the first to pick up the hoarse hooting of the Chevrolet horn. She shouted to the servant,

" Ranga, open the motor shed ! " Ramani as a rule sounded his horn at about a furlong from his gate, two long hoots which were meant to tell the household, " Ranga, keep the shed door open when I reach there, if you value your life," while to Savitri it said, " It is your business to see that Ranga does his work properly. So take warning." Some days the hooting would be less emphatic, and Savitri's ears were sufficiently attuned to the nuances and she could tell a few minutes in advance what temper her husband was in. Today the hooting was of the milder kind. It might mean that he was bringing home a guest for dinner or that he was in a happy mood, possibly through a victorious evening at the card-table in his club. In either case they could await his arrival without apprehension. If he was happy he treated everyone tolerantly, and even with a kind of aggressive kindness ; if he had a guest, he attended on him with such persistence and concentration that he would not notice the failings of his family. Savitri had a qualm for a moment, because a guest would mean a great deal of messing about with oil and frying-pan and stove and getting some extra dish ready within the shortest possible time. Ramani was never in the habit of an-nouncing in advance the arrival of a guest or of tolerating any poor show in the dining-room. He just picked up a friend at the club and brought him home for dinner. It made him furious if it was suggested that he should give notice : "We are not so down-and-out yet as not to afford some extra food without having to issue warnings beforehand."

"But if we should have a lot of food left over every day?" Savitri had asked once or twice.

"Throw it into the gutter."

"Or we can give it to the beggars?" Savitri suggested.

"Certainly. By all means. Make it a rule every day to give some food to the beggars. Remember, if I see any beggar turned away from our door, I shall be very wild."

Savitri, however, had other methods of dealing with sudden guests. She had a genius for making the existing supply elastic and transforming an ordinary evening course, with a few hurriedly fried trimmings, into a feast.

Today, however, the soft hooting was not due to the presence of a guest. Savitri was greatly relieved to see her husband come into the house alone from the shed. Her alternative inference that he was in a happy mood was confirmed by the fact that he did not pass off into the right wing of the house with bent head, but stood at the doorway wiping his shoes on the mat and looking about. Again he did not say to Savitri, " See if the fellow has locked the garage door," but merely asked, " Have the children had their food ? " And again, after going to the room he did not shout in the dark, " Who is trying to save the electric bill by keeping the house as dark as a burial-ground ? " but quietly switched on the lights.

Savitri felt relieved ; the same relief ran through the children, who were all at their desks in another room, waiting, keyed up. They had now caught the signals. Ah, Father was going to be pleasant. It meant they could just hang about the dining-hall and listen to their elders' talk ; otherwise they would have had to keep to their books for some time and then crawl away to their pillows.

After undressing and changing, Ramani came very quickly towards the dining-hall and said to Savitri, " Hope you have finished your dinner."

" Not yet."

" What a dutiful wife ! Would rather starve than precede her husband. You are really like some of the women in our ancient books."

" And you ? " Savitri asked. She could take any liberties with him now. She could say anything. She could be recklessly happy and free.

"I? I'm like—you'd have to write a new epic if you wanted anyone like me in an epic." And he laughed and patted her on the back. She understood what it meant : he would make love to her, a kind of heavy, boisterous love, even before the cook and the children.

While eating he caught sight of Babu lurking behind the door, and said, " Hallo, you are still alive ? The way your mother protected you this morning I thought——"

" My headache left me in the afternoon, Father."

" Certainly, so that you might not miss the cricket in the evening ; isn't it so ? " Babu was silent. Ramani persisted in asking till he confessed that he went to cricket in the evening.

" Look here, young fellow. I've been your age and played all these dodges in my time. So you can't trick me," said Ramani, and turned to Savitri. " Which of us was right ? "

Savitri blushed. " The boy did have a headache in the morning," she said, and felt ashamed of herself for her excessive concern.

" Listen," Ramani said to Savitri. " Bear this in mind. There is a golden law of headaches. They come in time for school and leave in time for cricket." He laughed heartily, well pleased with his epigram. Babu tiptoed away. Ramani said to Savitri : " You have to learn a lot yet.

15

You are still a child, perhaps a precocious child, but a child all the same."

The beginning of love-making—Savitri understood and changed the subject. "What happened to Ramaswami? You never told me what you did with him."

"Oh, him? We disposed of that affair a long time ago. I didn't want to report the fellow to the head office. I called him up and warned him. He has made good the amount."

"You won't get into trouble for that?"

"Trouble? Isn't it enough if I don't get them in to it? After all, he's only a poor fellow. Some temptation. A small amount. He has a good record of service."

"But they may not like your disposing of the question so easily?"

"If they don't like it, here is Mr. Ramani's resignation, and you can look out for another secretary for your blessed branch."

"And suppose they accept the resignation?"

"Madam, the Engladia Insurance Company is a big one, I admit, but it is not the only insurance company in the world. Before I took charge, Malgudi District was not giving them even ten rupees' worth of policies a year, and now ten lakhs of business is passing through my hands every year. What do you say to that?"

Savitri's tactics never failed. If she wanted

to divert his attention she had only to work him up into a professional mood. He was going on, expatiating on his work, on the offers he received from other companies, and so on. It saved her from his romantic attentions till the two girls came in.

" Ah, dear lady," Ramani said to Kamala. " Why have you neglected us ? "

" I was doing my lessons."

" Lessons ! Lessons ! You are a great woman. Didn't you hear your father come home ? "

" Yes, Father."

" That's all you care for us poor folk," Ramani said with an elaborate mischievousness. " What about you, lady ? " he said, turning to his first daughter. " Ah, how serene you look ! You already look as if you had grandchildren." The children giggled and looked at each other and giggled again. Savitri laughed. He would have been hurt if she hadn't. Ramani looked at his daughters benevolently and then looked at his wife and said with a wink, " I wonder which of them will grow up like you ? In any case, if any of them become half so— h'm, h'm ! as you are . . . I rather like the way you have arranged the jasmine in your hair today."

Savitri said, rising, " Get up. Time to go and wash our hands."

Chapter Two

THOUGH Savitri was on visiting terms with about a score of houses in the South Extension, she had only two real friends—Gangu and Janamma.

Savitri found Gangu fascinating. She had humour, abundant frivolity, and picturesque ambitions. She was the wife of a school teacher, and had four children. It was her ambition to become a film star, though she lacked any striking figure or features or acting ability ; she wanted to be a professional musician, though she had no voice ; she hoped to be sent some day as Malgudi delegate to the All-India Women's Conference ; to be elected to various municipal and legislative bodies; and to become a Congress leader. She spent her days preparing for the fulfilment of one ambition or another. For serving on public bodies she felt she ought to know a little more English than she needed to read fairy tales and write letters to her husband at the beginning of their married life. Hence she engaged a tutor, who made her go through Scott's novels and trained her in conversation by putting inane questions to her in English. She prepared for her film career by attending two Tamil pictures a week and picking up several screen songs, in addition to wearing flimsy crêpe *sarees* and wearing her hair and flowers in an eccentric manner. She talked irresponsibly and enjoyed being unpopular in the elderly society of South Extension. She left home when she pleased and went where she liked, moved about without an escort, stared back at people, and talked loudly. Her husband never interfered with her but let her go her own way, and believed himself to be a champion of women's freedom ; he believed he was serving the women's cause by constantly talking about votes and divorce.

Gangu was tolerated in the Extension : she was interesting ; with all her talk, she was very religious, visiting the temple regularly, and she was not immoral.

Savitri's other friend, Janamma, was a different type altogether. She was rotund, elderly, and rich. Her husband was a Public Prosecutor. She never moved very freely among people. Savitri had a great regard for her, and consulted her whenever she was seriously worried.

Savitri was friendly with both Janamma and Gangu, though the two found each other intolerable. Janamma said of Gangu, " That restless rat," and Gangu said of Janamma, referring to her size and deportment, " That temple chariot." Janamma asked Savitri, " Why do you allow that silly pup to worry you with her company ? " Gangu often asked Savitri, " How do you manage to remain alone with that creature? Isn't her face frightening at close quarters ? She looks like a head-master we had when we were at school."

Between these two implacable enemies Savitri maintained a subtle balance. Only once did she find herself in a very difficult situation— when both of them met in her house. It happened that Gangu was on a visit to Savitri's house and Janamma dropped in later in the evening. Savitri was sitting on the bench in the hall with Gangu by her side. At the sight of Janamma, Gangu lost her voice but was too proud to get up and go away. Janamma stopped short as if a trap had caught her foot. Savitri said, " Ah, come in, *mami*," and edged away a little and made space for her on the bench on her other side. The enemies sat one on each side of her. There was an uneasy silence. Savitri made a vacuous remark on the heat during the day. The remark was in danger of extinction without a response. Shuddering at the prospect of having to invent another equally innocuous, Savitri turned to Gangu and asked anxiously, " Didn't you feel it ? "

" Yes, I did," replied Gangu cheerlessly.

Savitri, fearing that she might appear to be bestowing more attention on one than on the other, quickly turned to Janamma and inquired, " It's unusually hot for the time of year, isn't it ? "

" I suppose so," said Janamma.

Then once again silence. Savitri felt the whole situation was thoroughly ridiculous—all three sitting on the same bench side by side like school children, and only one being able to talk. Janamma suddenly rose from the bench and sat on the floor, muttering an explanation, " I always feel more comfortable on the floor." Savitri found herself in a dilemma : she couldn't sit on the bench herself while an elderly visitor was sitting down on the floor, and she couldn't leave Gangu for the other. Savitri solved the problem by getting up, moving away from the bench, and standing at a spot which wasn't too near to either Gangu or Janamma. Gangu stared fixedly at a picture on the wall and Janamma kept looking at the door, and Savitri stood completely baffled. How was this to be brought to an end ? Neither was willing to be the first to leave. Savitri kept on talking as best as she could of that day's menu for breakfast, the price of vegetables, scarcity of good vegetables, the impudence and avarice of some vegetable-vendors, the difficulties of going to the market every day, and all the bother with servants and cooks. She had to talk looking at neither in particular, and standing. She was invited twice to sit down, and twice did she complain of acute discomfort at the knee-joint.

This terrible situation only came to an end by the passage of time. It was nearing seven and Janamma could not stay any longer because it was time for the Public Prosecutor to return home and she would have to be there. When she was gone Gangu said triumphantly, " Did she think that I would be afraid of her and scramble out of the house ? "

Chapter Three

SAVITRI was in Janamma's house one evening when Kamala came and said, " Father wants you to come home immediately."

" Father ! Has he come home ? "

It was very unusual. Savitri's heart beat fast. Was he terribly ill ? Or had anything happened to him or to the house ? Why had he not gone to the Club? " Why has he come home so soon, Kamala ? "

" I don't know, Mother. I was playing in Kutti's house when he called me up and told me to find you at once. I couldn't stop and talk to Father : he looked so angry."

Savitri rose, saying to Janamma, " I must be going." She almost ran out of the house. Kamala went prancing before her. " Why don't you walk like a normal female, Kamala ? You will break your neck some day."

" Mother, shall we see which of us can reach home first ? "

When she turned into her street, she saw that the car was still parked in the road. " Didn't he tell you why he wants us so urgently ? " she asked, and Kamala shook her head and said,

" He was very angry that Sumati and Babu were not at home."

" How can the children be at home in the evenings ? Doesn't he know that they have to go out and play ? "

Savitri's throat went dry at the sight of her husband. He was pacing the front veranda ; he had changed his coat and was wearing a blue blazer. He looked fixedly at her as she came up from the gate and said, " You have made me wait for half an hour." He added, " A fellow comes home from the office, dog-tired, and he has only the doors and windows to receive him. Where is everybody gone ? Anyone could walk in and walk out with all the things in the house."

" I left the cook in charge of the house."

" He is not a watchman. Perhaps you'd like him to put up his oven at the street gate so that he can look after the house and cook at the same time."

Her suspense had relaxed. He wasn't ill, and nothing else was wrong anywhere. She knew that he was either going to tell her that he was dining out or ask her to go out with him in the car. He said, looking at his watch, " It is getting late. Are you coming with me to the cinema or not ? "

" Now ? "

" Immediately."

24

"Where is Sumati, Kamala? Babu will be in the field. Send Ranga to fetch them while I dress."

"The children can go some other day. Not a fly extra now."

"Oh," she said unhappily. She knew it would be useless to plead. All the same she could not restrain herself. "The poor things, let them come, they will enjoy it." Kamala was already making some indistinct impatient noises.

"It is very bad for the children to be taken out every time their elders go out."

"At least let Kamala come with us," said Savitri.

"Father, let me come to the cinema too."

"You must never ask to be taken out."

"If I don't ask, nobody will take me out," said Kamala, and turned to her mother: "Please let me come too. Sumati and Babu won't mind."

Ramani was infuriated at the sight of the girl appealing to her mother and thundered, "Learn not to whimper before your mother." To Savitri he said, "Are you coming out at all or shall I go alone? You can stay here and pet the little darling."

"Let us go some other day," she said.

"No. I want you to come now. Children

some other day. I have not come all the way to be told ' Some other day.' I am not a vagabond to come in and go out without a purpose. Go and dress quickly. It is already six-fifteen. We can't fool about on the veranda all day."

Savitri went in. Kamala went behind her, showing symptoms of stamping her feet and crying. Ramani said, " If I hear you squeal, I will thrash you, remember. Be a good girl." He shouted a moment later, " Savitri, I will count sixty. You must dress and come out before that." Instead of counting sixty he went on talking ; " Women are exasperating. Only a fool would have anything to do with them. Hours and hours for dressing ! Why can't they put on some decent clothes and look presentable at home instead of starting their make-up just when you are in a hurry to be off? Stacks of costly *sarees*, all folded and kept inside, to be worn only when going out. Only silly-looking rags to gladden our sight at home. Our business stops with paying the bill. It is only the outsider who has the privilege of seeing a pretty dress."

§

Malgudi in 1935 suddenly came into line with the modern age by building a well-equipped theatre—the Palace Talkies—which simply brushed aside the old corrugated-sheet-roofed Variety Hall, which from time immemorial had entertained the citizens of Malgudi with tattered silent films.

Ramani sat in a first-class seat with his wife by his side, very erect. He was very proud of his wife. She had a fair complexion and well-proportioned features, and her sky-blue *saree* gave her a distinguished appearance. He surveyed her slyly, with a sense of satisfaction at possessing her. When people in the theatre threw looks at her, it increased his satisfaction all the more, and he leant over and said, " They are showing *Kuchela*."

" Yes. I read the notice while coming up."

" It is a Tamil film. I thought you would like it." He spoke to her because he was in a position to do it, and it made him feel important. He enjoyed his rôle of a husband so much that he showed her a lot of courtesy, constantly inquiring if her chair was comfortable, if she could see the screen properly, and if she would like to have a sweet drink.

The hall became dark and the show began. Savitri, like the majority of those in the hall, knew the story, had heard it a number of times since infancy, the old story from the epics, of Krishna and his old classmate Kuchela, who was too busy with his daily prayers and meditation to work and earn, and hence left to his wife the task of finding food for their twenty-seven children. . . .

Everything was there : Krishna's boyhood ; he and his gawky classmates waylaying curd-sellers and gorging themselves. A feat it was to consume so many pots of curds. An endless procession of rustic women with pots on their heads passed under the trees, in the branches of which a gang was waiting ; the women halted under the trees and nearly asked to be robbed of their pots. How they wrung their hands at the broken pots and chased Krishna. As the curds spread on the ground, " What a lot of curd wasted ! " Savitri could not help thinking. And then Krishna's classroom jokes and the various ways in which he tormented his monitor ; nobody was in a mood to question why the monitor, a perfectly timid and harm-less man, deserved this treatment. Savitri en-joyed the sight of the troubled monitor and the triumph of the saucy-looking Krishna so much that she laughed aloud and whispered to her husband, " Babu should have seen this, he would have enjoyed it."

" Don't keep bothering about Babu, other-wise you won't be able to enjoy the show," said her husband.

She was enchanted by the picture. It ran for nearly four hours. The film people had shown no hurry : they had a slow, spacious way of handling a story which gave a film-fan three times his money's worth. There were songs which characters sang as long as they liked, there were scenes of " domestic humour " which threatened to last the whole evening, a procession complete with elephants and pipers and band that took half an hour to pass, a storm which shook the theatre, a court scene with a dancer which was an independent programme by itself ; there were irrelevant interludes which nearly made one forget the main story.

Savitri sympathised intensely with the un-fortunate woman, Kuchela's wife. " The poor girl ! " she muttered to her husband.

" Note how patient she is, and how un-complaining," Ramani remarked.

Savitri was embarrassed by a suggestive conversation between a very fat husband and his wife at bedtime ; she was thrilled by the magnificence of the procession ; and she was immensely pleased when in the end Krishna heaped on his old friend wealth and honour. The whole picture swept her mind clear of mundane debris and filled it with super-human splendours. Unnoticed by her passed the fumbling and faltering of the tinsel gods and the rocking of the pasteboard palaces in the studio wind, and all the exaggeration, emphasis, and noise. The picture carried Savitri with it, and when in the end Kuchela stood in his *pooja* room and lighted camphor and incense before the image of God, Savitri brought her palms together and prayed.

The first show ended at ten o'clock.

The switching-on of the lights, the scurry of feet, and a blue-coated husband yawning, had the air of a vulgar anti-climax. " You must bring the children tomorrow," she said. The old Chevrolet groaned and started. She loathed the dull drab prospect of changing her *saree*, dining, and sleeping. The night air blew on her face and revived her earthly senses a little. As she sat beside her husband, she felt grateful to him and loved him very much, with his blue coat and the faint aroma of a leather suitcase hanging about him.

When she reached home, she found Ranga and the cook sitting up in the front veranda. Sumati and Babu were there too. Kamala had slept on the hall bench. " The poor girl has fallen asleep on the bench ! " exclaimed Savitri. " Have the children had their food ? Did Kamala cry long after we went ? Babu, you must see this picture. It is very good."

" An Indian film ! " sneered Babu.

" You must see the little boy who acts Krishna. How can a small boy act so well ! He is wonderful."

Babu smiled indulgently. " That shows you have never seen Shirley Temple. They pay her one thousand pounds a week to act. If you see *Curly Top* you will never like any other picture."

" Mother, he has not seen that picture. He is lying," said Sumati.

" I never said I saw it. A friend of mine has seen it twice, and he told me all about it."

" You see this picture and then say. Your father has promised to send you all to it to-morrow."

" I don't like Indian films, Mother. I would like to be sent to *Frankenstein*, which is coming next week," Babu said.

" I don't like English films. Let us go to this tomorrow," Sumati said.

" It is because you don't understand English films," said Babu.

" As if you were a master of English and understood all that they say in the films ! Why do you pretend ? " said Sumati.

This threatened to develop into a quarrel, but Savitri stepped between them and said, " Sh ! Don't start fighting."

Chapter Four

In the month of September the streets rang with the cries of hawkers selling dolls—the earliest intimation of the coming *Navaratri* festival.

" Mother, aren't we buying some dolls this year for the festival ? "

" What's the use of buying them year after year ; where are we to keep them ? "

" In the next house they have bought for ten rupees a pair of Rama and Seeta, each image as large as a real child."

" We have as many as we can manage. Why should we buy any more ? "

" Mother, you must buy some new dolls."

" We have already three casks full of dolls and toys."

A day before the festival the casks were brought into the hall from an obscure storing-place in the house. Ranga had now a lot of work to do. It was an agreeable change for him from the monotony of sweeping, washing clothes, and running errands. He enjoyed this work. He expressed his gay mood by tying a preposterous turban round his head with his towel and tucking up his *dhoti*.

" Oh, look at Ranga's turban ! " screamed Kamala.

" Hey, you look like a cow," added Sumati.

" Do I ? " Ranga bellowed like a cow, and sent the children into fits of laughter.

" Don't waste time in playing. Open the casks and take out the dolls," said Savitri.

Ranga untied the ropes and brought out the dolls in their yellowing newspaper wrappings. " Handle them carefully, they may break." In a short while dust and sheets of old newspaper, startled cockroaches and silverfish were all in a heap on one side of Ranga, and, on the other, all the unwrapped dolls. Most of them had been given to Savitri by her mother, and the rest bought by her at various times. There they were—dolls, images, and toys of all colours, sizes, and shapes ; soldiers, guards, and fat merchants ; birds, beasts, and toys ; gods and demons ; fruits and cooking utensils ; everything of clay, metal, wood, and cloth.

Ranga in his preposterous turban, stooping into the casks and bringing out the dolls, looked like an intoxicated conjurer giving a wild performance. The children waited, breathlessly watching for the next item, and shrieked at his absurd comments : " Ah, here is my friend the parrot. He pecks at my flesh." He would suck the blood on his finger and vow to break the parrot's beak before the end of the festival. He would hurriedly take out and put down a merchant or a grass-seller, complaining that they were uttering terrible swear-words and that he couldn't hold them. He would pretend to put the toy foods into his mouth and munch them with great satisfaction. Or he would scream at the sight of a cobra or a tiger. It was pure drama.

Savitri squatted down and wiped the dust off the dolls, and odd memories of her childhood stirred in her. Her eyes fell on a wooden rattle with the colour coming away in flakes, with which she had played when she was just a few months old. So her mother had told her. There was a toy flute into which she had wasted her babyhood breath. Savitri felt a sudden inexplicable self-pity at the thought of herself as an infant. She next felt an intense admiration for her mother, who never let even the slightest toy be lost but preserved everything carefully, and brought it all out for the *Navaratri* display. Savitri had a sudden longing to be back in her mother's house. She charged herself with neglecting her mother and not writing to her for several months now. . . . How frightfully she (Savitri) and her sister used to quarrel over these dolls and their arrangements! She remembered a particular *Navaratri* which was completely

34

ruined because she and her sister had scratched each other's faces and were not on speaking terms. Poor girl ! Who would have dreamt that she would grow into a bulky matron, with a doctor husband and seven children, away from everybody in Burma? That reminded her, she had not answered her letters received a month ago; positively, next Thursday she would write so as to catch the Friday's steamer.

Now Ranga had put down a rosy-cheeked, auburn-haired doll which was eloquent with memories of her father. She remembered the evening when he had awakened her and given her the cardboard box containing this doll. How she adored this cardboard box and the doll and secretly used to thrust cooked rice into its mouth and steal sugar for it ! Poor father, so decrepit now ! . . .

A crash broke this reverie. Ranga had dropped a bluish elephant, as large as an ordinary cat.

" You ass, did you fall asleep ? "

" Oh, it is broken ! " wailed Sumati.

" Make him buy a new one, Mother. Don't give him his pay," suggested Kamala.

Savitri felt very unhappy over the broken elephant: it was one of a pair that her mother had got from *her* mother, and it had been given to Savitri with special admonitions, and not to her sister, because she could not be depended upon to be so careful, and Savitri's mother had been very reluctant to separate the pair. . . .

" I told you to be careful," Savitri said. " and yet, you ass——"

Ranga picked up the broken elephant. "Oh, madam, only its trunk is broken," he announced gleefully.

" What is left of an elephant when its trunk is gone ? " Savitri asked mournfully.

Ranga stood examining the trunkless elephant and said : " It looks like a buffalo now. Why not have it in the show as a buffalo, madam ? "

" Fool, stop your jokes."

" He doesn't care a bit ! " Kamala said, horrified.

Ranga said to Kamala, " Little madam, I know now how buffaloes are made."

" How ? " asked Kamala, suddenly interested.

" By breaking off the trunks of elephants," said Ranga. Then he said, " Allow me to take this home, madam."

" Impossible," said Kamala. " Mother, don't let him take it. Tell him he must pay for it."

" It is broken. Why do you want it ? " Savitri asked.

" My little boy will tie a string round its

neck, drag it about, and call it his dog. He has been worrying me to get him a dog for a long time."

Kamala said, " You won't get it," and snatched the elephant from his hand.

Now all the dolls and toys were there, over five hundred of them, all in a jumble, like the creations of an eccentric god who had not yet created a world.

Babu had given definite instructions that the arrangement of the platform for the dolls was to be left entirely to him, and they were to do nothing till he returned from school. The girls were impatient. " It is not a boy's business. This is entirely our affair. Why should we wait for him ? "

Babu burst in at five o'clock and asked, looking about impatiently, " Have you put up the platforms yet ? "

" No, we are waiting for you. There is no hurry. Eat your tiffin and come," said Savitri.

In two minutes he was ready to do his work. The girls jeered : "Are you a girl to take a hand in the doll business ? Go and play cricket. You are a man."

" Shut up, or I will break all the dolls," he said, at which the girls screamed. Babu hectored Ranga and sent him spinning about on errands. With about eight narrow long planks, resting on raised supports at the ends, he constructed graduated step-like platforms. He pulled out of the rolls of bedding in the house all the white bedsheets and spread them on the planks; he disturbed all the objects in the house and confiscated all the kerosene tins and stools, etc., for constructing supports for the planks. He brought in bamboo poles and built a pavilion round the platform. He cut up strips of coloured paper and pasted them round the bamboo poles and covered their nakedness. He filled the whole pavilion with resplendent hangings and decorations. He did his work with concentration, while the two girls sat down and watched him, not daring to make the slightest comment; for at the slightest word Babu barked and menaced the speaker. He gave Ranga no time to regale the company with his jokes, but kept him standing on a high table in order to execute decorations on the pavilion roof.

In a couple of hours a gorgeous setting was ready for the dolls. Babu surveyed his work from a distance and said to his mother, " You can arrange your knick-knacks now." He turned to his sisters and said, " Move carefully within the pavilion. If I find you up to some mischief, tearing the decorations or disturbing the plat-forms, you will drive me to a desperate act."

Savitri said to the girls, pointing to the

pavilion, "Could you have made a thing like this ? You prated so much when he began the work." Sumati was a little apologetic and appreciative, but Kamala said, " If you had given me a little paste and paper I too could have done it. It is not a great feat." Savitri said, " Now lift the dolls carefully and arrange them one by one. Sumati, since you are taller than Kamala you will arrange the dolls on the first four platforms, and, Kamala, you will do it on the lower four platforms. Don't break anything, and don't fight."

In an hour a fantastic world was raised : a world inhabited by all God's creations that the human mind had counted ; creatures in all gay colours and absurd proportions and grotesque companies. There were green parrots which stood taller than the elephants beside them ; there were horses of yellow and white and green colours dwarfed beside painted brinjals ; there was a finger-sized Turkish soldier with not a bit of equipment missing ; the fat, round-bellied merchant, wearing a coat on his bare body, squatted there, a picture of contentment, gazing at his cereals before him, unmindful of the company of a curly-tailed dog of porcelain on one side and a grimacing tiger on the other. Here and there out of the company of animals and vegetables and mortals emerged the gods—the great indigo-blue Rama, holding his mighty bow in one hand, and with his spouse, Seeta, by his side, their serenity unaffected by the company about them, consisting of a lacquered wooden spoon, a very tiny celluloid doll clothed in a pink *saree*, a sly fox with a stolen goose in its mouth, and a balancing acrobat in leaf-green breeches ; there stood the great Krishna trampling to death the demon serpent Kalinga, undistracted by the leer of a teddy bear which could beat a drum. Mortals and immortals, animals and vegetables, gods and sly foxes, acrobats and bears, warriors and cooking utensils, were all the same here, in this fantastic universe conjured out of coloured paper, wood, and doll-maker's clay.

" It is all very well now, but the trouble will be in putting them all back carefully after nine days in their casks. It is the most tedious work one could think of," said Savitri.

" Mother, don't dismantle them again. Why can't we let them stay out for ever ? It is always so terribly dull when the decorations are torn down and the dolls are returned to the casks."

§

Next morning Babu took a look at his work and decided to improve it. It was all very well as far as gum and paper could go, but the lighting was defective. All the illumination that the pavilion got was from the bulb hanging a few yards from it in the hall. He would get his friend Chandru in, and fix up a festoon of ornamental coloured bulbs under the pavilion arch ; he would transform the doll pavilion into something unique in the whole of Extension.

He brought Chandru in the afternoon. Chandru was very much his senior, but Babu spent much of his time with him. Chandru was studying in the Intermediate and had a genius for electricity. He had made miniature dynamos, electric bells, and telegraph sets.

Sumati and Kamala were delighted. " It is going to beat the pavilion in the Police Inspector's house," they said ecstatically. Chandru worked wonders with a piece of wire and a spanner. In a short while he had created a new circuit with an independent switch. When the switch was put on, a festoon of coloured bulbs twinkled in the archway and two powerful bulbs flooded all the dolls with a bluish light.

" When you switch on in the evening, do it very carefully," warned Chandru, and left.

It was a great triumph for Babu. He felt very proud of being responsible for the illumination. " If you like I will ask him to come and add an electric train to the dolls. That will be wonderful," he said.

At five o'clock the two girls worried Babu to put the lights on. He told them he knew the right time to do it and warned them not to go near the switch. " Lighting at six," he said.

" We will be out at six," they protested, " inviting people. A lot of our friends will be coming now to invite us to their houses, and we would so love to have the illuminations at once. Please."

" Will you leave that to me or not ? I know when to do it, and I want you to mind your own business now."

Savitri said to Babu, " Don't be so strict. You have done everything for their sake, why should you grudge them the light now ? "

" All right, at five-thirty," said Babu.

At five-thirty nearly a dozen visitors had already arrived. Everyone wore bright silks, and sat gazing at the dolls. Finding so many ladies sitting in the hall, Babu hesitated at the door, wondering how he was to reach the switch in the pavilion. He called Sumati and said, " With the tip of your finger push that small rod to one side, to the left. You must do it very gently."

Sumati pushed the switch gently, then less gently, and then Babu shed his shyness and dashed to the switch. He rattled it, but nothing happened. Not only were the pavilion lights not on, but the usual hall bulbs had also gone out. Babu looked at Sumati and said, " I knew that if I let you touch it something or other would happen." He stood contemplating the new circuit, rattled the switch once more and said that somebody had tampered with it and that he would get at that person soon. Muttering that one couldn't plumb the depth of mischief in girls, he walked out of the hall. Nobody yet realised that anything was wrong because there was good sunlight.

At about seven-thirty the conditions were different. There was no light in the house. Visitors were received in the pale light of a hurricane lantern, and the pavilion was lit by flickering oil-lamps transferred from the *pooja* room. The atmosphere was dim and gloomy. The sisters' rage knew no limits. " Mother, do you understand now why we did not want any boy to come and interfere in our business ? As if it wouldn't have been a pretty sight without those lights. Who wanted them anyway? We never asked him to come and fix the lights."

Babu was in utter despair. Chandru had gone to the cinema and would not be back till nearly ten. And he had no friend who knew anything about electricity.

" Send someone to the Electric office," said Savitri.

" Shall I go ? " asked Babu.

Savitri hesitated. How could she send him out all alone so late ? " Take Ranga with you."

And protected by Ranga's company, Babu set out to the Electric office in Market Road— a distance of about two miles.

Babu stood before the entrance to the Electric office and said to someone, " There is no light in our house in the South Extension."

" Go in and tell it to the people you will find there."

Babu went in and was directed to a room in which three fellows were sitting, smoking and talking. One of them asked him, " Who are you, boy ? "

" The lights are out in our house in the South Extension."

" Put the switches on," somebody said, and all three laughed.

Babu felt awkward, but the light had to be set right. He pleaded : " Can't you do something ? We have tried the switches."

" Probably the fuse has gone. Have you seen if the meter fuses are all right ? "

" I haven't. There is nobody in the house."

" Then, why do you want the lights? If the meter fuse is burnt, it is none of our concern.

44

We will come only when the pole fuse is burnt. Go and see if the meter fuse is all right."

When Babu reached home he found his father had already arrived. He was in a terrible temper. Ranga's absence delayed the opening of the garage door and had infuriated him. In that state he entered the house and found it dark. Now failure of electric current was one of the things which completely upset him. He stood in the doorway and roared, " What is this ? " Savitri let the question wither without an answer. The girls did not dare to answer. " Is everybody in this house dead ? " he asked.

Savitri was angered by this, " What a thing to say on a day like this, and at this hour ! I have seen very few who will swear and curse at auspicious times as you do."

" Then why couldn't you have opened your precious mouth and said what the matter was ? "

" There is nothing the matter. You see that there is no current and that there are no lights, and that's all that's the matter."

" Has anybody gone to the Electric office ? "

" Babu has gone there."

" Babu, Babu, a very big man to go."

This irrational pointless cynicism enraged Savitri, but she remained silent.

Ramani passed in to undress, grumbling all

45   D

the way. Standing in the dark, he cursed the whole household and all humanity. " Ranga ! here, Ranga ! " he howled in the dark.

" I told you Ranga had gone to the Electric office with Babu," Savitri said.

" Why should everybody go to the Electric office ? Is Babu to be protected like a girl ? Whose arrangement is it ? " He raved, " Bring some light, somebody."

Savitri sent the hurricane lantern along with Kamala. Kamala set the lamp on the floor while her father looked at her fixedly. " Here, that's not the place to put the lantern. Do I want illumination for my feet ? Bad training, rotten training." He lifted the lantern and looked about for a place and said, " Don't you know that when you bring a lantern you have to bring a piece of paper to keep under it ? When will you learn all this ? "

" Very well, Father," Kamala said, much intimidated by his manner.

This submissiveness pleased Ramani. He said, " You must be a good girl, otherwise people won't like you." He placed the lantern on the window-sill. Kamala turned to go and took a few steps. " Little girl, don't shuffle your feet while walking," said Ramani.

" Hereafter I will walk properly, Father."

He was thoroughly pleased with her. He felt

46

he ought to bestow on her some attention—honour her with a little conversation. " Have you been in the dark all the evening ? "

" No, Father, we had current till six o'clock and then——" She hesitated.

" What happened ? "

" Babu's friend put up new bulbs for the dolls, and when Babu pressed a switch something happened, and all the lights went out."

When Babu returned from the Electric office he found his father standing in the hall and shouting. As soon as he sighted Babu he asked, " You blackguard, who asked you to tamper with the electric lights ? " Babu stood stunned. " Don't try to escape by being silent. Are you following your mother's example ? "

" No, Father."

" Who asked you to tamper with the electric lights ? "

" I didn't touch anything. I brought in Chandru. He knows all about electricity."

His father moved towards him and twisted his ear, saying, " How often have I asked you to keep to your books and mind your business ? "

" I'll try to set it right, Father, as soon as Chandru comes home."

" Who asked you to go near the dolls' business ? Are you a girl ? Tell me, are you a girl ? "

This insistent question was accompanied by violent twists of the ear. Babu's body shook under the grip of his father's hot fingers. " No, Father, I am not a woman."

" Then why did you go near the dolls ? " He twisted the other ear too. " Will you do a thing like this again ? Tell me ! "

In helpless anger Babu remained silent. His father slapped him on the cheek. " Don't beat me, Father," he said, and Ramani gave him a few more slaps. At this point Savitri dashed forward to protect Babu. She took him aside, glaring at her husband, who said, " Leave him alone, he doesn't need your petting." She felt faint with anger. " Why do you beat him ? " was all that she could ask, and then she burst out crying. At the sight of her tears, Babu could not control himself any longer. He sobbed, " I didn't know . . . I didn't know it was wrong to add those lights."

Ramani left, remarking that he was sick of this sentimental show. He came back after a wash. " Now to dinner. We will manage with the available lights." Savitri squatted down, her face covered with her hands. " I see that you are holding a stage-show. I can't stand here and watch you. Are you coming in for food or not ? . . . All right, you can please yourself." He turned and walked to the dining-room call-

ing, " Has that effeminate boy eaten ? Babu,
come for your dinner ! "

When he was gone, Savitri rose, went to the
dark room next tothe store, and threw herself on
the floor. Later the cook tracked her down there
and requested her to take her food, but she
refused. The children came to her one by one
and tried to coax her. She turned her face to the
wall and shut her eyes.

§

The next morning the cook brought her a
tumbler of coffee. She drank it. The cook took
back the tumbler from her hand and asked
nervously, " What shall I cook ? "

" Don't ask me," she said.

" There are only a couple of potatoes. We
will have to send for some vegetables and also
for some mustard."

" Do the cooking without the vegetables and
the mustard or go and ask whoever is keen
on having them for money. Don't come and
mention them to me."

The cook went away, his head bent in per-
plexity. Had anybody heard of cooking without
mustard ? Presently he got over his despair and
began to enjoy the excitement of the situation.
A part of his mind said, " Go on, prepare the

sauce and everything without mustard, and with only two potatoes, and if the master raves, tell him I waited long enough and gave sufficient notice." Another part of him said, " Look here, this is an opportunity provided by the gods. Show them your worth." In the backyard Ranga was splitting firewood. The cook said to him, " When the master and the mistress quarrel it is we that suffer."

" Not many words passed between them last night," Ranga said. " All the same, the situation appears to be very serious."

" It is no business of a wife's to butt in when the father is dealing with his son. It is a bad habit. Only a battered son will grow into a sound man."

" My wife is also like that," admitted Ranga. " I have only to look at my son and she will pounce on me. Last year when I went to the village my first boy did something or other. He skinned our neighbour's son's forehead with a sharp stone, and what should a father do ? "

" You will have to run up to the shop now and bring vegetables," said the cook.

" Certainly, but listen to this now," persisted Ranga. " What should a father do ? I merely slapped the boy's cheek and he howled as I have never heard anyone howl before, the humbug. And the wife sprang on me from somewhere and hit me on the head with a brass vessel. I have sworn to leave the children alone even if they should be going down a well. Women are terrible."

The servant-maid who was washing the vessels under the tap looked up and said, " Wouldn't you like to say so ! What do you know of the fire in a mother's belly when her child is suffering ? "

The cook said, " Only once has my wife tried to interfere, and then I nearly broke her bones. She has learnt to leave me alone now. Women must be taught their place." With this he dismissed the subject and turned to the immediate business on hand. " I'm responsible for the running of the house today. I'm going to show these people what I can do. The mistress of the house said, ' Do anything, don't ask me,' and I could well cook a dinner that a dog wouldn't touch. But is it a proper thing to do, after having been in the house for five years ? Ranga, it is eight o'clock. Master will be coming for food in about two hours. Run to the Nair's shop and buy onions for two annas, potatoes for four annas, two lemons, coriander for one pie. . . ." He knew what his master liked, and he was out to provide it. " Tell the Nair that he will get the money by and by."

Kamala went to her mother and asked,

"Mother, are you still angry?" Savitri did not reply.

"Father won't beat Babu again. Please don't go on lying there." She hated to see her mother in this condition, during the *Navaratri* of all times. "Mother, what sweets are we preparing for distributing in the evening?"

"We'll see," said Savitri.

This reminder pained her. She cursed her own depression of spirits, which threatened to spoil the festival. "I don't like these quarrels," Kamala said, and left her. She felt indignant. Her school was closed so that they might remain in the doll-land, visit each other, and eat sweets; but Mother went on lying on the floor with her face to the wall. She traced the whole cause of the trouble to Babu, and threw furious looks at him.

Babu went about without so much as looking at the pavilion. His whole manner declared, "This is what a man gets for helping in women's business. It is your school after all, not mine, that is closed for this silly festival. Please don't call me for anything." He was troubled in mind about his mother. It was he who had received the slaps, so why should she go on lying there as if a great calamity had befallen the house? Perhaps he ought not to have cried like a girl. The memory of his tears hurt him now.

He loathed himself and resolved he would never cry again in his life. Before starting for school he went to the dark room and said to his mother, " Why do you go on lying there ? It was only a slight slap that he gave me after all. You make too much of it. I am going to school now."

" Have you taken your food ? " she asked.

" Yes, get up and go about your business."

Ramani came in for food at his usual hour, before going to the office. He decided to ignore severely his wife's absence. He was going to show her that sulking would not pay. He demonstrated his calm indifference by humming a little song, whistling loudly, and by talking to his daughters, whom he saw in the hall sitting near the pavilion. He looked at the pavilion with condescending appreciation and said, " You must not keep them in such a jumble. You must have all the animals in one line, all the human beings in another, and so on. What sweets are you distributing this evening to your friends ? "

The girls looked at each other and said, " We don't know yet."

" Don't you worry, I will buy sweets for two rupees." He raised his voice while saying it, which was a message to the dark room : " Don't imagine that the festival can be spoilt by your sulking."

He whistled as he entered the dining-hall. He asked the cook with a decided cheerfulness what he had prepared, and said " Very good " at the end of the list. The cook had prepared the meal very well because he had the run of the kitchen cupboard, and he had made unstinting use of rarities like pure ghee and parched coconut, while Savitri would have allowed him to use only gingelly oil and no coconut. Ramani ate his food with thorough enjoyment. He shouted suddenly to his daughters in the hall, " Kamala, did you eat plenty of this potato and onion stuff? "

" Yes, Father."

" Did your sister eat plenty of it ? "

" Yes, Father."

He then asked, " Aren't the sauce and the plantain chips excellent? " This was meant to convey to whomsoever it might concern that no one was indispensable.

The cook was very happy, which was due not only to his master's compliments but also to the fact that the freedom of the kitchen cupboard had enabled him to check his ten-thirty hunger with a gulp or two of curd.

Before leaving for the office Ramani called the girls and said, " On my way I shall drop in at the Electric office and send someone from there. You will have lights this evening."

" Very good, Father. Can those coloured lights remain ? "

" All right, if you want them."

" But Babu said that he would ask Chandru to come and remove them today."

" Ask him not to. Tell him that I want them there. When the Electric man comes, ask him to see if they are all right."

Just as the engine started Kamala ran to the car and shouted above its din, " Don't forget the sweets."

" Certainly not," he said, and wished that his engine made less noise so that his words might be heard in the dark room.

§

At two o'clock the girls began to feel scared. Mother had refused food and was still lying in the dark room. Sumati sat before the pavilion and wondered what to do. Mother's absence gave the house a still and gloomy appearance. Kamala returned to the hall after her tenth visit to the dark room.

" What does she say ? " asked Sumati anxiously.

" She wouldn't answer me at all. ' What

jumper shall I wear this evening?' I asked, but she wouldn't answer."

"You are a fool," Sumati said. "You ask the same question every time."

"No. I've asked this question only three times. I've already asked her whom to invite this evening, when we are to go out, at what time to switch on the lights, and what sweets we are to have. I can't think of any more questions."

The children believed that, if their mother could be made to answer some question and get involved in conversation, she could then be persuaded to come out of the dark room. This was a diplomatic step, but Savitri's answers were discouragingly to the point, and when she understood the purpose of the questions she stopped answering them.

"Why don't you go in and try?" suggested Kamala.

"Impossible," replied Sumati. "I'm afraid of anyone who lies in a dark room with her face to the wall." She presently thought out a plan. "I know how to get Mother out of this fearful state."

Kamala was delighted, though she did not yet know what Sumati meant to do.

"I may have to go out for a moment," Sumati said. "I shall be back very soon. Look after the house and don't tell anyone that I am out."

The mysterious air which she gave to the whole business thrilled her. Kamala became excited. " Where are you going ? "

Sumati hesitated and asked, " Will you swear that you won't tell anyone ? "

" I never swear. Isn't it enough if I tell you that I will keep the secret ? "

" No," said Sumati, and rose to go.

" I will come with you," Kamala said.

" No. You will stay here."

" Then I will go in and tell Mother that you are going out of the house."

" If you do that, I will not go out and Mother will remain in the dark room for ever."

Kamala was in despair. " By our gods I swear I will not tell anyone where you have gone. Now tell me."

" I am going to Janamma's house to bring her here. Mother will listen to her words."

Kamala was doubtful. " But don't you think that family secrets should not be allowed out of the house ? "

This was a reasonable objection. Sumati remained thoughtful and said, " I will merely tell her that she had better come and see Mother at once, and nothing more."

" Do you think there will be anything

wrong in it if you just mention that Babu spoiled the electric lights last night? I don't think if you merely asked her to come she would come."

Janamma was enjoying a siesta on a mat in the front room of her house. Sumati stood on the edge of the mat silently. She hesitated for a moment whether to wake her up or not; left alone the *mami* would probably sleep till six in the evening. What was to happen to Mother? She leant over and softly called, " *Mami! Mami!* "

"Oh, Sumati! Come on, child, what do you want?"

" *Mami*, you had better come and see Mother at once."

"What's the matter with her?"

"I don't know."

"Is she ill?"

"I don't know. Perhaps."

"What is she doing?"

"She may be sleeping. You must come at once and ask her to get up and bathe and eat."

"Savitri," Janamma said, standing over her in the dark room. Savitri opened her eyes. She took a few seconds to identify the visitor.

" Ah, come in, *mami*. Sit down. Bring a mat, Kamala."

" I don't want a mat. I can sit on the floor. Do you know what the time is ? It is past two, yet I see that you have not had your bath or food. What is the matter ? "

Savitri said, " I am not feeling well."

" Is this where the sick people of your house usually sleep ? Look here, child, I am your senior ; you can't deceive me. When Sumati came and told me, I knew at once what it was. Don't contradict me."

" Why did that girl run up to your house and trouble you ? "

" What else could the poor thing do ? When the elders quarrel it is the children who really suffer."

" There is no quarrel. I never uttered a single word."

" That makes it worse. You should either let your words out or feel that everything your husband does is right. As for me, I have never opposed my husband or argued with him at any time in my life. I might have occasionally suggested an alternative, but nothing more. What he does is right. It is a wife's duty to feel so."

" But suppose, *mami*, he beats the child savagely ? " Savitri explained the situation.

59

"Men are impetuous. One moment they will be all temper and the next all kindness. Men have to bear many worries and burdens, and you must overlook it if they are sometimes unreasonable."

"I don't mind any treatment personally, but when a child——"

"After all they are better trainers of children than we can be. If they appear sometimes harsh, you may rest assured they will suffer for it later." Janamma went on in this strain for an hour more, recounting instances of the patience of wives : her own grandmother who slaved cheerfully for her husband who had three concubines at home ; her aunt who was beaten every day by her husband and had never uttered a word of protest for fifty years ; another friend of her mother's who was prepared to jump into a well if her husband so directed her ; and so on, till Savitri gradually began to feel very foolish at the thought of her own resentment, which now seemed very insignificant.

"Get up, Savitri. Bathe, and wear your best *saree* and take your food. You are a sight."

Savitri murmured something about still being unwell and not wanting food.

"I am not going to leave this place till I see you out of this room," Janamma said decisively.

Savitri needed only a little more persuasion, and when Janamma said, " What a foolish, inauspicious thing to do on a *Navaratri* day ! " she felt guilty of a great crime. And then Janamma said, " You are spoiling the happiness of these two girls. After all, *Navaratri* only comes once a year."

Savitri hated herself for her selfish gloom.

" Girls, your mother wants to bathe. See if there is hot water."

" I'll ask the cook to get it ready in a moment," Sumati said, and ran out. Kamala ran behind her, almost dancing with joy. She screamed to the cook, " Hot water ! Mother is coming out of the dark room ! "

Chapter Five

IN the New Year the Engladia Insurance Company decided to take a few women probationers into its branches, who were to be trained in office and field work, and later assist the Company in securing insurance policies on female lives. The Company advertised its new scheme with the maximum noise, and the response was very satisfying.

A large number of applications poured into Ramani's office. " We are not anxious to adorn our establishment with so many of the fair sex ; we are more anxious to have them in as policy-holders," he observed with a dry official humour to Pereira, his office manager.

" What shall we do with these applications, sir ? "

" Call them up for interview between the fifteenth and twentieth instant. We can fix up the number of interviews per day accordingly."

" Many of them have to come up from other towns, sir."

" They must come at their own expense."

" A nice treat the boss has arranged. You

can have your pick for the harem between the fifteenth and the twentieth. Don't miss the office on any account," he said to Kantaiengar, the Accountant.

"Wouldn't it be enough if I kept my head above water with the family I have?" said Kantaiengar. He strongly disapproved of the new scheme. "Do they want to convert the Company into a brothel?" he asked.

"A delightful idea," Pereira remarked.

To Ramani, too, the scheme appeared novel and fantastic, but the Head Office at Madras pursued it with zest, and Ramani had to sit up and interview a lot of women between the fifteenth and twentieth of January. Out of the thirty or forty women he interviewed every day he couldn't find one that seemed to him likely to do any work for the Company. Some of them were just girls, educated up to Matriculation or Intermediate, young and bashful and pitifully trying not to give an impression of being too young or bashful. Some were widows, some were prostitutes out to take up a spare-time occupation. Ramani felt that these women would in no way add to the profits of the Company, though they added considerable colour to the office on the days when they were present. Kantaiengar bent over his accounts more than ever, resenting this intrusion and feeling self-conscious ; the other clerks looked intimidated. Pereira made a festival of it. He arranged their accommodation in a spare corner of the office and flirted with them elegantly.

Ramani went through the interviews in a state of boredom, irritated with his Head Office for this infliction. He told the applicants after a number of questions that they would hear from him in due course.

On the very last day the last applicant entered. At the sight of her Ramani pushed his chair back and rose—a thing he had not done for anyone till now. Pereira, who followed the applicant in, delicately whisked his moustache with his little finger, and showed that he noticed this difference.

" Sit down, please," Ramani said, and resumed his seat only after the visitor had sat down. He cleared his throat and asked, looking at a list before him, " You are Mrs. Shanta Bai ? "

" Yes," she said.

He looked at Pereira who was hovering about, and Pereira gave another delicate whisk to his moustache and made an unobtrusive exit. Outside, he winked at Kantaicngar and whispered, " Of that *houri* in there we shall see a great deal, and, perhaps, hear also a great deal, yet."

"Which district do you come from?" asked Ramani.

"I'm from Mangalore," Shanta Bai said.

"Mangalore?" Ramani echoed, and added as a piece of courtesy, "Some day I have planned to visit your district."

"Oh," she said, "but it is a pretty dull place. I'm sure you won't like it."

Ramani felt that he had been snubbed, but presently he appreciated the candour and smartness which had released the snub. He smiled and replied briskly that he was grateful for the timely warning, otherwise he would have wasted some money and time in going to Mangalore. She received the remark without interest. Ramani felt hurt. He suddenly asked himself angrily, "Who is the master here?" Abruptly he shed all his unofficial humanity and asked severely, "Do you live with your people there?"

"It is a difficult question, and it will take a lot of answering."

Ramani once again felt his official manner slowly melting. He gathered himself together and said, "I see you are married."

"I am," she said in a pathetic low voice, and Ramani did not dare put to her further questions about her private life. He said apologetically, "I'm sorry to trouble you with personal questions, but I have to send a report to the Head Office. If they appoint you they will want to know all about you, whether your family is likely to hinder you in your work——"

" Oh, of that you can assure them. If I had a family to hinder me I shouldn't have come here with my application."

" I shall want some more details and facts," implored Ramani. While, till now, all the interviewers had been at his mercy, he found himself, to his distress, at the mercy of this applicant. He liked her pluck. Very seldom, he told himself, did such fair lips utter words without affectation or timidness. He admired her manners very much. She said as if taking pity on him, " Well, here is my life story. I was born in Mangalore. I was married when I was twelve to a cousin of mine, who was a gambler and a drunkard. When I was eighteen I found he wouldn't change, and so I left him. My parents would not tolerate it and I had to leave home. I had studied up to the Fifth Form, and now I joined a Mission School. After completing my matriculation, with the help of an aunt, I came to Madras and joined the Women's College. I passed my B.A. three years ago. Since then I have been drifting about. I have had odd teaching jobs and I have also been companion to a few rich children. On the whole it has been a very great struggle. It is all non-sense to say that women's salvation lies in education. It doesn't improve their lot a bit ; it leaves them as badly unemployed as the men."

" I am really surprised to hear it," said Ramani, feeling it was time he said something.

" So must anyone be, most of all we ourselves. We struggle hard, get our B.A., and think that we are the first of our kind ; but what happens ? We find that there are thousands like us."

Her tone was soft and pleasing. Ramani wanted to ask her if she could sing well, but restrained himself and said, " Yours is a very interesting story. Then I suppose you saw our advertisement ? "

" Yes, I did. I sent my application to all the branch offices, and I was called up for inter-view only by you."

" Where were you at the time ? "

" I was in Bangalore, staying with some old college friends and looking for work. Now I am here. If you find me suitable for your office, I will be for ever grateful to you."

A thrill went through Ramani's being ; this beautiful creature grateful to him ! He swelled with importance as he said, " I will do my best for you. Of course you know the final decision rests with the Head Office. I will do my very best for you."

"Thank you very much," she said.

"I must also tell you now," he began in the orthodox style of the senior to the probationer, "that an insurance career is not at all an easy one. It is one of the most exacting professions in the world. I've been in it for a decade and a half now. . . ." The banalities and autobiography lasted till Pereira came in with a bundle of papers in his hand.

§

Ramani learnt that she lived in a hotel. That simply would not do. He called in Pereira next day and asked, "What are you doing with that room in the passage?"

"Nothing very definite, sir. We have thrown in a few old chairs and records."

"Can't you transfer that lumber to some other place, and make it habitable? Mrs. Shanta Bai is staying in some dirty hotel; why shouldn't we give her that room till she gets settled in this place? There is no harm in it."

"Oh, none whatever, sir."

"It must be rather awkward for a lady to live in a hotel, you see."

"You are right, sir. No decent hotel in the whole town. I will have the lumber turned out and stocked somewhere else. But the records?

68

They are rather important. What about keeping them here ? "

" Here ? " Ramani didn't like the idea of anything intruding in his room. " Put them away in some other place."

" All right, sir. You will want the room ready tomorrow ? "

" Yes, as soon as you can attend to it, thank you."

Outside, Pereira told Kantaiengar, " I shall have to fix up a nuptial chamber in the office, Iengar."

" What is he driving at ? It is absurd. This will be the talk of the town."

" I am sure it will bring more people into the office."

The other members of the staff also resented this feminine intrusion because a lot of lumber was brought into their room ; and the old office watchman resented it because the passage room had been for years his home.

§

Ramani asked at home, " What happened to the spare cot we had ? "

" Krishnier's people borrowed it months ago when he was down with rheumatism, and they have not returned it."

" Send for it. I want it for the office. We are going to fit up a guest's room."

" What for ? "

" We get a lot of outsiders ; some important people come to us on business now and then, and we have to provide them with some decent accommodation."

" If it is for the office, buy a cot with your office money. Why should we give ours ? " She dared to suggest this amendment because it was one of his good-humoured evenings.

" But look here, my girl. If it comes to that, everything in this house, including the grain in the storeroom, belongs to the office, bought with the office money, you know." She argued elaborately that they were not living on the charity of the Company, and declined to lend the cot. He pleaded and cajoled her. He liked to plead and cajole this evening. He said, " I shall want it only for a time. I will return it as soon as we buy new furniture. There is no time now. An important guest is coming tomorrow. I shall also want your bench, a chair, and one or two vessels."

" Oh, you want everything we have in the house." The teakwood bench was her favourite piece of furniture. " If you take away the bench, what am I to sleep on in the after-noons ? "

" Oh, I will get you velvet couches, my dear," he said, bringing his hands together in a romantic gesture. " There is nothing that I wouldn't buy for you. Only say it." It made her very happy.

§

The Head Office confirmed her appointment nearly a week later. Ramani's recommendation was so strong that the Head Office had no choice in the matter. Shanta Bai was to be on probation for six months, provided she did personal canvassing worth ten thousand rupees within the first two months (if she failed she was to be sent away and the next applicant on the list called up and given a chance). During the probationary period she was to receive a stipend of sixty rupees a month ; after that she was to have a starting salary of a hundred and fifty rupees a month, with commission, and work as the chief woman agent for the branch.

On the day the confirmation came, Ramani sent for Shanta Bai and dramatically pushed the letter before her. He tried to look casual and unconcerned. He went through some papers while she read it. Though pretending to look at the letters he was secretly noting how artistic her chequered jumper was, and awaited eagerly her thanks for all his trouble.

"I am rather disappointed," she said.

Ramani looked up, startled.

She said, "I thought the starting salary would be two hundred." She remained thoughtful for a moment and added, "I had no business to imagine it because the advertisement never mentioned the amount."

"What, is this girl going to reject the job for the sake of fifty rupees?" Ramani thought for a harrowing moment, and rushed to console her. "You seem to overlook the fact that you will be drawing two hundred in two years. Please read carefully that increment clause. Besides, you will be getting your commission over your actual salary."

"Well, I take your word for it. I will do whatever you advise me to do."

He was pleased with the importance she gave him, and sat reflecting for a moment. How well a simple voile *saree* sat on her! Why couldn't one's wife dress as attractively?

Shanta Bai said, "I thought that if I had a start of two hundred I could buy a tiny Baby Austin for myself." She added with a sentimental sigh, "But I suppose all one's dreams can never come true."

"I am sure your commission on your personal work will enable you to have even a big Austin with a driver and all. Shall I wire to the Head Office that you accept the terms and ask them to post the agreement immediately ? "

" As you please," she said.

Such an exquisite complexion came only from Mangalore, Ramani thought ; you could see the blood coursing in her veins. He said aloud, " I will see if the probationary period cannot be cut down, and if the stipend cannot be put up a bit. But that's all by and by. You may rest assured that your interests will have the best support and protection possible."

" Excellent ! When do I start work ? "

" Tomorrow. Now you can go ' home ' if you like." She rose and went out. Ramani looked after her and meditated. What a delightful perfume even after she was gone ! What an impotent, boorish beggar that husband must be who couldn't hold this fair creature ! What an innovation it would be to have a beauty on the office staff ! The town was sure to talk about it. He hoped her presence wouldn't be too upsetting for the office staff to go on with their usual work : they must get used to it. It was all nonsense to keep men and women separate in water-tight compartments ; women were as good as men and must be treated accordingly. He told Pereira, " The Head Office has confirmed the lady's appointment."

" It is pleasing news," Pereira said.

" She is starting work tomorrow. I want you to arrange a table, etcetera, for her somewhere. Where are we to put her up ? "

Pereira reflected for a moment and said, " There is plenty of space in the office. We can make some kind of arrangement, sir."

He had a vision of Kantaiengar : wouldn't it give him fits if he heard this ? Ramani asked, " Are you sure it wouldn't be an inconvenience ? "

" Not at all. We are only a dozen in that large hall." He paused, gave an elegant whisk to his moustache, and asked, " Are we to put up a screen ? "

" Is it necessary ? "

" I do not know, sir, but I thought that the lady might want it."

" Hm ! You can get the screen if you feel that she might be a distraction to the typists." He laughed as well as his official dignity would permit him.

Outside Pereira said to Kantaiengar, " Clean up your table and go to that corner. I will give you another table."

" What do you mean ? "

" Orders from the boss. The fairy is taking her seat here. She is to be given the best place, and so you have to quit."

" This is atrocious. I shall resign."

" And leave your family in the streets, I suppose ? "

" What does he mean by it ? "

" Women and children first, my dear fellow. A rugged piece of timber like you can be kept anywhere, but wouldn't a fresh rose need a lot of air, light, and this large table, to keep it alive ? "

Kantaiengar was wild. " Isn't it enough that he has dumped all that lumber here, making the place unsightly and choking, that he should be bringing in this thing now ? "

" The two are hardly alike except to your prejudiced mind. And that reminds me, we shall have to cover the lumber-heap with a Persian carpet when madam sits here."

" What I can't understand is why he is thrusting her here. Why can't he have her in his room, on his lap if he likes ? "

" All in due course. Meanwhile, may I tell you that the boss has asked me to arrange your chair to face a wall ? He said, ' Take care that the accountant does not lose himself in a trance and fail to add and subtract. Let his chair be arranged to face a wall.' "

" Does he take me for a woman-hunter like himself ? Remember that if only I cared for these things——"

" You could have had a hundred women at your beck and call ? Likely too. . . . Do you very much wish to stay where you are and not to be disturbed ? "

" I will resign this job before I move out of this place," said Kantaiengar furiously.

" We can't afford to lose you. So I will tell the boss not to worry you, if you promise you won't scowl at her when she is here. I don't see why you should be so sour. Personally, I rather welcome her ; something to relieve this drabness, you know. But it will be a difficult job, all the same, for me to see that the typists and others do their work. The boss said, ' Keep an eye on the typists, and on the Accountant.' "

Chapter Six

ONE evening while returning home from the Club Ramani passed his office in Race-Course Road, and had an impulse to stop his car and go in. He told himself that it would be improper, and passed on ; but the car had hardly run a few yards when he told himself that he ought to inspect his office periodically at nights. That would make the watchman more alert. He had also to see if the safe and the file-chest were locked properly. One read in the papers of all sorts of thefts and rifling in the offices. By this time his car had nearly reached the junction of the Race-Course Road with Market Road. He turned the car round and drove towards his office.

He found the watchman sleeping soundly at the foot of the staircase. Ramani stood over him, musing indignantly : " Fast asleep at eight o'clock ! I will speak to Pereira about it to-morrow." He climbed the stairs. He saw a light in the glass ventilator above the door of the room in the passage. He stood gazing at it for a moment and then passed into his office room. He switched on the lights, went over to the file-chest and the safe, and tugged at their locks solemnly. He then wondered what to do. His inspection was over. He pulled out his drawer and idly looked at some of the envelopes in it ; he spent some time pulling the pins out of the cushion and pushing them back ; he examined the nibs of the pens on the table, went over to the chest and safe, tugged at their locks again, switched off the lights and came out of the room. He descended two steps, saying that he must really be hurrying away : why keep Savitri and the servants waiting unnecessarily ? He paused suddenly, went up the two steps again, and gave a couple of gentle knocks on the door of the passage room.

" Who is that ? "

Ramani had a momentary confusion as to who he should say he was. He said, " Oh, don't disturb yourself. On my way home, I just remembered something and dropped in for a moment."

Shanta Bai recognised his voice and opened the door. " I was rather terrified, you know. Wondered if someone had come to abduct me."

" Abduct you ? " Ramani gave a slight inept laugh. " I just began to doubt if I had locked the safe in the evening. Rather worrying, you see, such doubts. It brings to one's mind all the accounts of thefts and safe-breaking that one reads in the papers. A troublesome business having such a responsibility on one's head."

" It must be awful. If anything goes wrong, I suppose you will be taken to task ? "

" I shall be sent to jail. Not a paper must be lost, not an anna must escape the accounts."

She listened to him with her eyes sparkling in the light of the bulb hanging in the passage. She was dressed in a white *saree*, and had jasmine in her hair. She asked abruptly, " Why do you stand in the passage ? Won't you step in ? "

" I thought you might think it a bit unconventional."

" Oh, I love unconventional things," she said. " Otherwise I shouldn't be here, but nursing children and cooking for a husband. Come in, come in, see how I have made a home for myself."

Ramani stepped in, pleasantly excited, marvelling at Shanta Bai's ability to adapt herself. How meekly she accepted his official aloofness which he was of late practising in the office, and how warmly she now responded to a little friendlness ! She had put up a few printed *khaddar* hangings on the doors and windows, a few group photos of her college days on the wall, a flowery counterpane on her bed, and a silk cushion on the chair. The door of an antechamber was covered with a curtain. " She does her toilet and dressing in there," Ramani thought with an inexplicable thrill. He looked about and exclaimed, "What a transformation!"

"Please sit down."

"Not when a lady is standing," Ramani said.

"All right," she said, and went over to her cot and sat on her counterpane. He sat down on the teakwood bench. She threw up her arms and stretched them, saying, "My joints are becoming stiff. I think I am getting old."

Ramani treated this remark as a great joke and laughed.

"Do you mind if I don't sit erect?" she asked.

"Oh, not at all, make yourself comfortable."

She reclined on her pillows, stretched her legs, and said, "I can't sit up. Even in my college days I used to lie in bed and study all night."

Ramani's eyes followed every minute movement of her limbs. She tossed her head now and then, slightly pouted her lips, and raised her brow. Ramani felt now that his stiff aloofness with her during the office hours was a piece of cruelty and that some explanation was due to her: "I have just remembered to tell you—if you have found me a little different in the office, please don't be hurt."

" Oh no. Nothing can hurt me. In the office you are the chief, and now——"

" Your brother, if you will permit me to say so."

"You have my fullest consent to think of me as your sister."

" Oh, it is very good of you. In the office I don't want anyone to notice any difference. That's why I try not to give them any impression that my treatment is different——" He fumbled on elaborately.

After conferring on him the privilege of brotherhood, she grew intimate in her talk. The account of her life with her harsh husband was really moving. Ramani listened for a second time, with absorbing interest, to her account of her struggles after leaving home. He said that men deserved to be whipped when she hinted at a couple of attempts on her honour. He was in complete agreement with her philosophy of life (which cropped up at the end of every ten minutes thus : " As for me life is . . ." something or other, some simple affair like Living Today and Letting Tomorrow Take Care of Itself or Honour being the One Important Possession, and so forth). He had known all these himself, but they had a new value for him when they issued from those fair lips. He assured her of his very best help when she told him what she hoped to achieve in the services of the Company. And bang into all this philosophy, autobiography, and hopes came the office clock's chime.

" It can't be ten ! " he exclaimed, pulling out his watch. " I thought it was just eight-thirty or nine." He rose with a sigh.

" If I had had the slightest idea you were coming, I would have kept some food for you," she said. " It is very wrong of me to have kept you so long and to turn you out now on an empty stomach."

She went down the stairs, and walked up to the car to see him off. He started the car and suddenly asked, " Would you like a drive ? "

" Now ? "

" Yes, why not ? "

" Aren't you hungry ? "

He made a noise deprecating the idea of hunger, and suggested that a drive around with his sister would be more than food to him.

" No, I will really not trouble you now. I should have loved a drive if you had eaten something."

He was deeply touched by her consideration and said : " I had a very heavy tiffin at the Club. I don't think I can eat anything tonight."

" Why have you stopped the engine ? "

" The car won't start."

" Really ? What is wrong ? "

" It needs another passenger besides myself to make it go," he said.

She laughed at the joke and asked him if he was going to wait there all night till he could get a passenger. Yes, he said, with fervour, even if it was going to keep him there all night ; and added, " I suggest that we go round Race-Course Road, and then, if you don't mind, to the river. Have you ever seen it at night ? "

" Is it a very lovely sight ? "

" Come and see it for yourself," he said.

" You don't mind the trouble ? "

" Don't ask ridiculous questions."

She went up to lock her room. Ramani took out his handkerchief, dusted the seat lightly, got down, and waited for her. She came back to the car, and opened the door of the back seat. " No, not there," he said. " Don't you see that the door is open here ? "

" I prefer the back seat," she said.

" You do, I am sure, but the engine won't start unless there are two passengers in the front seat. You are not afraid of me, are you ? "

" Certainly not," she said, and climbed in. He sat beside her and drove the car. The engine heaved, sputtered, and settled into a steady rattle, and above it she said, " Aren't the stars in the sky beautiful ? How delightful the night

air is when it rushes on one's face ! " She tossed
her head and took a deep breath.

" Yes, yes," he agreed with her, and asked,
" Are you fond of moonlit nights or dark
nights ? " feeling that he wanted to express
something poetic himself.

At two o'clock he went home. He drove the
car into the garage with as little noise as possible, opening the gate and then the garage
door himself. He felt rather irritated after-
wards, when he walked back into the house
from the garage. " I am not a thief getting into
a house," he said to himself, and loudly knocked
on the door, calling "Savitri, Savitri !" a dozen
times before she could get up from her bed and
come to the door.

She was still half-asleep as she followed him
to his room and asked, " Have you dined ? "
He threw an angry look at her drooping,
nodding figure and said : " I suppose you are
too sleepy to serve me. You need not have sent
the cook away. Sometimes a man may have to
return home late. One can't always be rushing
back, thinking of the dinner. Why do you send
the cook away at night ? You give the servants
unheard-of privileges."

Savitri shook off her sleep, went to the
kitchen, and switched on the light.

§

Ramani was beginning to feel worried. Shanta Bai had been in the office now for a month and yet she exhibited no aptitude for canvassing work. The Head Office seemed to be fanatical in regard to the clause laying down the minimum of work to be done in the first two months. They had just sent a reminder. If Shanta Bai did not complete the amount in a month, she would have to be dismissed. Ramani looked down the list and noted that there was a Sharadamma of Gavipuram next to her. Would *she* have to be called up ? It was a distasteful thought. When Pereira next came into the room Ramani said, " Will you please ask the lady probationer to come in a moment ? "

Shanta Bai came in. " Please sit down," Ramani said. " You have been here for a month now. Do you feel you will be able to do ten thousand rupees' worth of canvassing in another month ? "

" I hope to. Otherwise I suppose I shall be turned out ? "

" It is a pretty rotten condition, I agree, but the Head Office sticks to it. Ten thousand rupees for two months is not very high either. I am rather worried because I have just received a reminder. I would advise you to reduce your office work and go about with the chief canvassing agent a little more. I will ask the office to relieve you of some portion of the work you are at present doing. That's all, thank you."

She went to her table with bent head. Pereira followed her and asked, " A troublesome interview ? "

" A reminder from the H.O." She told him about it. " What a horrid business to get the women of this town to insure ! They simply won't do it. Either they do it or I walk out of the office."

" If I may make a humble suggestion, madam, you may succeed better if you see the men themselves and persuade them to insure their wives."

She turned over a few papers piled upon her table and said, " Mr. Kantaiengar, here are some accounts papers, I am sure brought by mistake. Please take them away."

" Madam, from today you will try to learn something of the accounts too. Will you kindly check the figures in those papers ? "

" I will do nothing of the kind. The boss said he would relieve me of office work for some time."

" I was instructed yesterday to put you through the accounts. You can do what you please. Those are merely accounts of the daily agency reports. If you care to check the figures, it will be for your own benefit. Otherwise you can send the papers back to me tomorrow, but till tomorrow they will have to be with you whether you look at them or not. I can't disobey the instructions that I have received. Thank you."

" What a wicked ruffian ! " Shanta Bai whispered to Pereira.

§

On the way home from the Club Ramani halted at the office. This was threatening to become a daily habit. It was almost impossible to go home direct from the Club. Even the Club clung to him as a habit, perhaps as a necessity too—one had to leave the office premises at the closing of the day. At the Club he cut short his bridge a great deal nowadays, and never went near the billiard table. He left the Club early, put in a little unofficial attendance at the office, gave Shanta Bai a drive, and went home at ten at night.

Shanta Bai was in a bad mood today. The afternoon's interview had upset her. " What a riddance it will be for you in a few weeks," she said as soon as he came in and took a seat. She compressed her lips and jerked her head in

87

the perfect Garbo manner: the temperamental heroine and the impending doom. Ramani had to be the soothing lover. He went near her and patted her shoulder gently. Shanta Bai refused to be comforted. She revelled in the vision of a blasted future. "I know my fate, and I will not shirk it." Ramani told her that he would somehow persuade the Head Office to cancel the troublesome clause. "Don't be absurd," she said. "I won't have you do anything special for me."

She freed herself from his arms and paced the room up and down. "You shan't make yourself the laughing-stock of the Company," she said. She was steadily, definitely, methodically working herself up to a breakdown. Ramani knew it. He had already experienced it twice. She would start thus, and then sit with her face on the pillow, slight tremors shaking her back. In a moment she would rise, draw herself up, jerk her head and laugh at herself and at her moods. Such moments were very painful to Ramani. More than the breakdown, the subsequent heroic effort to master it stirred him deeply. He had never seen such things before; his wife's moods were different. She knew only one thing, a crude sulking in the dark room. She never made an effort to conquer her moods; that was why, he felt, women must be educated;

it made all the difference. He felt unhappy at
thinking disparagingly of his wife. Poor girl,
she did her best to keep him happy and the
home running. He told himself that he was
not criticising her but only implying that with
a little education she might have been even
better.

Shanta Bai went through her breakdown
act and was just about to jerk her head and
laugh at herself ; Ramani rushed at her, locked
her in his arms, and implored her to be
courageous. She released herself from his arms
and said : " Tonight I feel like pacing the whole
earth up and down. I won't sleep. I feel like
roaming all over the town and the whole
length of the river. I will laugh and dance.
That's my philosophy of life. Laugh, clown,
laugh—it was a film I saw years ago. Laugh,
clown, laugh, though your heart be torn," she
said, unable to quote the exact words of the
film. She asked suddenly, " Shall we go to a
picture tonight ? " This was the first time she
had suggested this, and Ramani sat more or
less stunned. " I said shall we go to a picture
tonight ? " she repeated with emphasis.

" Tonight ? " Ramani asked in weak apprehension. There were already rumours abroad,
and now to be seen together in public . . .

" Tonight. Answer in a word, yes or no."

"Certainly, certainly," Ramani said. "I was just wondering what the picture was and if it was worth a visit. What is the picture tonight?"

"Whatever it is, I must see a picture to-night. If you are not coming with me, I am going alone. If you are coming, I am prepared to share my food with you." She added, "Perhaps you don't wish to be seen in public with me; perhaps your wife will object; perhaps——" All of which suggestions he indignantly repudiated. He asserted with much bravado that he cared not a straw for public opinion, and that his wife was not the sort to question him or dictate to him.

He dallied till nine-thirty, when the picture should have started, so that he might make an unobtrusive entry into a dark hall and take his seat inconspicuously.

When they reached the theatre, she looked at the posters and exclaimed, "A wretched Indian film! I'd have given my life to see a Garbo or Dietrich now."

"What shall we do?"

"Anything is better than nothing." She sat in the dark hall beside him, whispering criticisms of the picture before her: a stirring episode from the *Ramayana*, in which the giant monkey god set fire to Lanka. . . .

"What rubbish the whole thing is!" she said. "Our people can't produce a decent film. Bad photography, awful acting, ugly faces. Till our film producers give up mythological nonsense there is no salvation for our films. . . . Let us get out. I can't stand this any more."

Ramani followed her out. In the car she asked, "Shall we go to the river?"

"Yes," Ramani said.

"It is only ten. Let us sit on the bank and stay there till the dawn," she said, and laughed as if she had uttered a huge joke.

Ramani laughed faithfully and drove the car towards the river. She sat nestling close to him as he drove, and said suddenly, "Let us drive round the town once and then go to the river." Ramani stopped, reversed, and drove the car into the town and about the streets. "I'm rather mad tonight," she said. "I hope you don't mind it."

"Not at all," he said.

After driving the car along the principal thoroughfares of the town Ramani asked, "What shall we do now?"

"To the river, to the river. You have a mad woman beside you tonight." After about an hour at the river she suggested going back to her room. "I can't sleep tonight," she said as soon as she got down at Race-Course Road. "Would you care to step in? Shall we sit up and chat till dawn?"

"With pleasure," Ramani said, and followed her into her room.

He returned home at five o'clock next morning. Savitri was in the veranda, watching the milkman milk the cow. When Ramani came up the veranda steps, she said, "I was very anxious all night."

"Oh?" he said.

"I wish you had sent word or something. Where have you been?"

"Can't you wait?" he cut in petulantly. "Do you want me to stand at the street door and shout my explanation?" Savitri stepped aside and let him pass into the house.

She stood looking at the milkman, listening to the sound of milk squirting into the pail. Suddenly the sound ceased: the milkman looked up and asked, "Master seems to have gone out very early today." It stirred a disturbance in her mind. She tried to kill the question with her silence, but the milkman would not be silenced. He repeated, "Master seems——"

Savitri replied, "Yes. He had to go out very early in the morning to see someone."

§

At about eight o'clock she took a tumbler of coffee and made it an excuse to meet her husband in his room. He was just back from a bath and was combing his hair. He saw her in the mirror but pretended not to have seen her. She saw his face in the mirror and doubted if any effort at peacemaking would be possible now. She hesitated whether she should place the coffee on the table and go away or should venture to ask a question. For the last few days disturbing doubts and a dull resentment had been gathering in her mind, and she hated herself for it. She felt angry with him and unhappy at being angry. It sapped all her energy. She would have given anything to lighten her mind of its burdens and to be able to think of her husband without suspicion. Just a word from him would do, just an unangry word ; even a lie, a soothing lie. Unpleasant thoughts seemed to corrode her soul.

She set the tumbler on the table, threw a glance at the person engaged in hairdressing so intensely, and decided that it would be better to suffer in silence than to venture a question. She started out, turned once again at the threshold, caught him looking at her with a side glance. " Shall I go out ? " she asked, turning to him. Ramani pretended to be absorbed in his own thoughts. She said, " I have put the tumbler on the table," and went out. She saw the maidservant standing uncertainly about. " Why are you idling there ? " Savitri asked. " Perhaps you are manœuvring to ask for something or other, that you want the afternoon off and so on. If you want to absent yourself in the afternoon you had better absent yourself for ever. I can get scores of persons like you."

" Why do you shout at me, my lady ? What have I done ? "

" I will shout as I please. You are not the person to question me. If you don't like it, you had better get out."

" Madam knows only one thing, and that is saying ' Get out ' for everything. I was only waiting to ask if I may go home."

" So soon ! Have you done all your work ? "

" Yes, madam."

" Scrubbed the back-yard ? "

" Yes, madam."

" Swept the whole house ? Washed all the vessels ? Have you removed the cowdung near the gate ? "

" Yes, madam, I have done everything."

" Why are you in such a hurry to finish your work and go home ? Home, home ; always

94

dying to return home. Dust and grime everywhere, at every corner. Now listen to this. You
shall not go home before ten from now on,
whether you have work or not. Understand
me? If you don't like it, you can get out this
moment."

The servant was an old woman who had
done a few years of service in the house and so
knew her mistress's moods. Savitri went in and
found everything in the kitchen irritating. " Is
this how you have been taught to slice brinjal?"
she asked, throwing a fiery glance at the cook.

" The brinjals were rather large——" began
the cook.

" Shut up, and don't try to invent an excuse
for every blunder you commit ! A set of useless,
blundering, wasteful parasites in this house ! "

Savitri went and sat on a carpet in the hall.
Sumati came out of her little study. " Why are
you sitting down, Mother ? " she asked.

" Why not ? When there was the bench I
could just rest on it for a moment when I felt
tired ; and now I have to squat down on the
floor every time. The bench is gone. Nothing
remains in this house. Everything has to be
sent away to the office. Go and tell your father
that I want the bench back immediately. He
is in his room. Go and tell him."

Sumati stood hesitating, and suggested

95

weakly, " Why don't you tell him that yourself,
Mother ? I'm afraid . . ."

" Afraid ! Everybody is afraid of him."

When he sat down for his dinner before
going to the office she hovered about, attending mechanically. He ate very quietly, fixedly
looking down at the rice on his leaf. She felt
a sudden pity for him ; there was something
pathetic in the quietness with which he had
accepted the ill-cut brinjals. Possibly Gangu
might have lied. It might be nothing more than
a scandal. The poor man was perhaps pouring
over account-books all night, and now without
a moment's rest he would have to be rushing
back once again in the hot day after heavy food.
All for whose sake ? She despised herself for
listening to gossip. After all these years of life
together, this was not the way to judge him.
She was not going to let her foul mind spoil
their life. She resolved not to ask him about the
bench. She resolved to re-establish peace. She
asked : " Wouldn't you like a little more rice
for the curd ? "

" No," he said.

She said, " Babu has scored sixty marks out
of one hundred in arithmetic. He stands fourth
in his class this term."

He displayed no enthusiasm over this news.
She said again : " I had a letter from my sister

96

in Rangoon yesterday. All are well there. It seems her husband's appointment was recently confirmed. And what do you think ? My sister says that she is expecting her eighth child in a few months."

" So your sister has gone far ahead of you ? " he remarked hollowly.

Savitri succeeded in making a few sounds like laughter. Though her bitterness was now gone, she felt still a little uneasy. What would she not have given to be coaxed and cajoled a little now ! All the same it was not so bad as it had been a few moments before.

When he was ready for the office she met him at the veranda steps. How well he looked in his silk suit ! It was sheer envy that must have made Gangu and the rest talk scandal about him, they with their husbands all crooked and paunchy. She mustered up all her strength and asked, " Will you be late tonight too ? " He frowned at her without a reply. She at once said apologetically, " I didn't mean to . . ."

" I can't be answering idiotic questions. You think I am just as old as Babu ? " He strode furiously towards the garage.

Gangu flitted in in the afternoon. Savitri was lying on the carpet in the hall reading her magazine.

" What has happened to the bench which used to be here all these days ? You are lying on the floor," asked Gangu, and unwittingly started once again the very thoughts that Savitri had been at pains to smother since the morning.

" Something or other has happened to it," Savitri said, discouraging all further reference to the subject.

Gangu said, " I just asked because the hall looks so bare without it. I felt perfectly disgusted with the home, and so threw everything up and came out. Sometimes I do get into such a mood, you know."

" I suppose you have finished the tiffin for the afternoon ? "

" That's just what I haven't done. I said to my husband when he started for the school, ' Don't expect any tiffin this evening when you come back from school. I would advise you to fill your stomach in a hotel.' "

" What about the rest at home ? "

" If he does not bring a packet for me and the children I will drive him out once again. He knows it."

" Well, what is the news in the town ? " asked Savitri.

" Nothing very special. Did you see the Tamil picture they are showing at the Palace ?

There are some good songs in it, but I could have played that heroine better. I will do it some day. Just wait. . . . I think your husband went to the picture."

" What ! "

" He was sitting two or three chairs off mine."

" So it was not the account-books that he had been poring over all night," Savitri thought.

" Didn't you know ? " Gangu asked.

" I don't usually bother him with questions as to his whereabouts."

" But didn't he tell you that he had been to the picture ? "

" He doesn't tell me anything unless I ask him ; and he was so terribly busy the whole morning that I couldn't get a word with him."

Savitri wanted all further talk about her husband to cease now, and switched on to, " I heard that you were about to make records of some of your songs."

" Yes, one of my husband's friends knows a person who knows some of the gramophone people in Madras. It is well under way. But it is all a secret yet."

Savitri thought : So he had not been poring over accounts all night. Perhaps he had to go out and meet someone in the theatre. Gangu said unasked, "Don't think I am gossiping, but there was another person with him ; perhaps it is that person about whom people are talking all this nonsense. I didn't want to tell you, but I thought you might as well know, because what harm is there ? "

Savitri sat gazing on the floor ; she couldn't speak ; she felt feverish. Gangu apologised. "You mustn't let it affect you so much. I wouldn't have mentioned it if I had known you would be so foolish."

Savitri still said nothing. The silence, to a person unaccustomed to it like Gangu, was very uncomfortable. She made a feeble effort to divert Savitri's thoughts by talking about the picture, its merits and demerits. Savitri did not lift her eyes from the floor. It was a monologue for Gangu. Savitri asked suddenly, " What was she like ? "

" Who ? the heroine ? They should have . . ."

" Not your heroine of the picture, but the real one."

" Forget her. Don't brood over it like a fool. There can't be anything in it."

" I must know what she was like. I never asked you to tell me about her. You have done it. Tell me everything. I must know ! "

" There is nothing for you to know, that's all."

" What was she like ? "

" She is an old woman, very ugly, and no man would go near her."

Savitri broke down. " I know you are lying. She can't be old. Perhaps I am old and ugly. How can I help it ? I have borne children and slaved for the house."

" No, no, you are a darling. You are beautiful. You aren't old."

Savitri said, " I am middle-aged, old-fashioned, plain. How can I help it ? She must be young and pretty. He has not been coming home before midnight for weeks. And yesterday he didn't come home at all ; came only in the morning, and wouldn't talk to me." She said, blowing her nose, " He is indifferent even to the children. Tell me everything ! "

Gangu wept a little herself and said, clearing her throat : " I won't hide anything from you. They didn't stay very long in the theatre. She said something and both of them went out at ten o'clock."

" And he couldn't come back home before the morning," added Savitri.

She asked, " Were they sitting very close to each other ? "

" Yes."

" Is she not young and better-looking than I am ? "

" Her skin is white, but who cannot make
herself up to look younger ? "

§

Savitri saw herself in the mirror in the
evening. Her eyes were swollen, her nose was
red. The girls came home from school. Kamala
cried, " Mother, your eyes are very red. Have
you been crying ? "

" No. Why should I cry ? I must have
touched my eyes with the fingers I used
for picking chillies, and I have a bad cold
too."

" Oh, I thought you had been crying, and
I was so terrified, you know. I thought Father
must have scolded you or something like that.
I do hate Father scolding you, because you
become so unhappy."

" Why should your father scold me ? He is
so good. He only scolds when I do something
wrong. How can one teach what is right without scolding ? "

" That's what our teacher says. If she raps
us on the knuckles when the arithmetic goes
wrong and we cry out, she says nothing can
be corrected without punishment. I am sure
it is all a lie. Can't a sum be set right without a rap on the knuckles ? "

"Mother, she gets thrashed every day at school," said Sumati.

"It's a lie. It is she that gets thrashed every day. Today our teacher sent me out to fetch a piece of chalk, and I saw Sumati in her class standing, and somebody said that her teacher had made her stand the whole period."

"It is a lie, Mother!" screamed Sumati. "I was standing because our teacher had asked me to give a dictation to the class. I'm not like you," she said, turning to Kamala.

They settled their differences very soon and went out to play. Babu came in from school. "Mother, I won't touch the tiffin unless you promise to give me my cricket fee tomorrow. I must give four annas to the captain."

"All right. I will give you the money."

"And I want a rough notebook tomorrow."

"You bought one only four days ago."

"Yes. It is all filled. Can't we buy even rough notebooks liberally? There is my friend Gopal. His people buy him one dozen notebooks every month, and here you grumble at buying even two."

After Babu left for the cricket-ground, Savitri went to the mirror and scrutinised herself in it once again. The swelling of the eyes had subsided a little now. She smoothed out her hair with her fingers, turned her head, and looked at herself sideways. " What is she like ? " she asked herself. " I'm not very bad, am I ? Perhaps she is very good-looking. What is wrong with my face ? These strumpets with their powder and paint ! Has she as clear a skin as mine without her paints ? " She remembered her husband's figure in the morning as he was dressed for the office. " Perhaps I'm not good enough for him. Let me admit my complexion has become rather sooty, and these dark rings under the eyes. I am getting careless about my hair, and braid it anyhow ; it's hardly his fault if he can't like my appearance very much."

She applied a little scented oil to her hair, and combed it with great care. She braided and coiled it very neatly. She washed her face with soap and water, and applied very lightly a little face-powder. She had given up using face-powder and scented oil years ago. She stood before the mirror, applied a little perfumed paste between her eyebrows and pressed a very elegant pinch of vermilion on it, and trimmed its edges with her little finger to make it perfectly round. He always liked the forehead marking to be a little large. She stood close to the mirror, with her nose almost touching the glass. She was more or less satisfied with her appearance, except for two stray strands of grey hair which she had just discovered ; she smoothed them out and tucked them cunningly into an under-layer. The glass clouded with the moisture of her breath ; she wiped the moisture and saw herself once again. Perhaps the other one's cheeks were rosy, and her hair thicker and longer. "My cheeks, too, were rosy and my hair came down to my hips before I had my two miscarriages and three childbirths. . . ." She went out into the garden and plucked some jasmine and red flowers, strung them together, and placed them in a curve on the coil at the back of her head—he always liked the red flowers to be interspersed with the white jasmine, and always admired the curved arrangement.

She wondered for a moment if she should dress herself in a new *saree* from the box ; he always liked to see her in the blue one. But that might be too much. She felt a little shy to dress so well for the home.

The children had finished their dinner. They stood round and admired her and asked if she had been to a marriage-house. "You smell lovely, Mother," Kamala said.

"I don't like scents," Babu said.

"Won't you coil my hair on my head like yours ? " Kamala asked.

"I don't like this tight coiling," Babu said,

" it makes the neck very ugly. I like the hair to fall on the ears a little."

" You can ask your wife to braid her hair loose," Savitri said.

" Don't talk rubbish, Mother. I am never going to marry."

When the children went away for their study and sleep, Savitri sat up, her heart in a flutter : would he come back tonight ? It would be impossible to bear it if he kept away again ; the perfume and flowers to be wasted ! She wrung her hands. She went to the mirror, stole another look at herself, and thought that if he saw her now he would certainly like her. Love her as boisterously as he had loved her in the first week of their marriage. . . . " No, no," she told herself. " He will not keep away tonight, not after I have asked him. He has great consideration for my feelings though he may appear rough outside. What did he say ?— ' can't be answering idiotic questions ' ; of course he couldn't answer a question like that. Where was any sense in asking a man if he would return home ? That was why he wouldn't waste his breath in answering such a question."

She sat up quite late into the night. When overcome by fatigue she lay down, keeping her head lightly on the pillow for fear that she might crush the flowers or rumple the hair. He might come any time and she wanted to meet him fresh as she was in the evening ; there was nothing more unsightly than rumpled hair and crushed flowers on one's head. . . . She dreamt that her husband came home, held her in his arms, and swore that he had been carrying about only a coloured parasol, and silly people said that he had been going about with a woman. . . .

§

And morning came. It was a Sunday and the children had no school. Their presence in the house was a check on Savitri's gloom. When she was alone and when the children's voices were not heard, her mind reverted to its obsession : he hasn't come, he hasn't come, he doesn't care for me now (before the mirror), perhaps she is better than I am.

At about midday Kamala asked, " Mother, what has happened to Father ? "

" He has gone out on business. He has so much work to do at the office."

" Wouldn't he want to eat anything, or sleep ? "

" No. When men have work they forget food, sleep, and home."

Babu said, " When I become a big man I will be a big officer, and I won't leave the office, but stay there night and day and do my work. I like being there so much."

"What about your wife and children?" asked Savitri. Babu bared his teeth in disgust and said, "Why do you always talk about marriage? I hate it. I am not going to marry even if it is going to cost me my life."

"Very well, but what about me?" she asked. "Shall I have to be at home all alone while you are away?"

"You! Oh!"

"You had forgotten me. Everybody forgets me. When you become a big man perhaps you won't even recognise your mother if you see her anywhere."

Babu swore that he would always be at his mother's side, which comforted Savitri a great deal.

Ramani's car snorted and hooted at the gate at about nine that night. The children were already in their beds; the servant had dropped into a sleep in some part of the house. Savitri went to the garage and opened the door herself. Ramani came in and quietly went away to his room. The house had assumed a gloomy silence after the children had gone to bed. Savitri went about with a flush on her face. She decided not to open her mouth till he should finish his dinner. She hovered about him when he ate, and attended on him, while the sleepy cook served the food. Half-way through the dinner he seemed to notice suddenly that she was before him. " Have you had your dinner ? "

" Yes," she said. " You want me to sit up and wait for you, do you ? " She was astonished at her own manner. Ramani looked up for a moment but said nothing.

When the cook had gone for the day, and she had shut the front door and put out the lights, she went to the bedroom, cleared her throat and said, " This sort of thing has to stop, understand ? " He was already in bed, with a novel shielding his face. He lowered the novel and scowled at her. " Don't talk. Go and lie on your bed."

" I'm not going to, till you promise to come to your senses." She stood firmly beside his cot.

" Hush, don't talk so loudly. You will wake up the children and the neighbours," he said.

" Ah, how considerate you are for the children ! " she said.

He sat up, understood the terrific force that a woman about to be hysterical could muster, and tried to take her hands and draw her nearer. She pushed away his hand, crying, " Don't touch me."

" No, no ! What's the matter with you, my

109   H

pet ? This is strange. What is wrong with you ? "

He tried once again to hold her hands, and she shook her hands free, violently. " I'm a human being," she said, through her heavy breathing. " You men will never grant that. For you we are playthings when you feel like hugging, and slaves at other times. Don't think that you can fondle us when you like and kick us when you choose."

He tried to treat it as a joke and laugh it off. " Very well, my dear. I grant here and now that you are a human being who can feel and think. All right. Now go to bed. I am sleepy."

His endearing tone for a moment won her ; his acquiescence momentarily satisfied her ; and she was pleased that he had tried to fondle her. She burst into tears and allowed herself to be drawn to his side. She sat on the edge of his bed sobbing, and when he said, " Now, now, be a good girl, don't ! Lie down, my pet," she felt that all her troubles had ceased, and blamed herself for exaggerating a little mistake that he might have committed.

She remained thus for a little while and, encouraged by his endearments, asked, " Now, will you promise not to go near her again ? " The first surprise was over, he had exhausted the little accommodation his nature was capable of, and he was once again his old self. He was

irritated by the question and said, " I don't
want you to dictate to me." She repeated her
question and he said, " Don't be a silly fool."
She understood the menace in his tone, drew herself away from him, and said, " So you refuse ? "

" Yes."

" You won't give up this harlot ? "

" Mind how you speak ! " His head throbbed
with anger.

" You are not having me and her at the same
time, understand ? I go out of this house this
minute."

" You can please yourself. Put out the light.
I want to sleep." He turned towards the wall.

He heard the banging of the door, turned,
and found that she had gone out of the room.
A terrific indignation welled up in him : so
she was trying to nose-lead him with threats
of leaving, like a damned servant ! She could
please herself, the ingrate. All the kindness and
consideration wasted on her. When his bank
balance was low he had somehow bought her
that gold-laced *saree* and jumper because she
desired it, and the diamond studs on her nose
. . . the ingrate ! He rose from bed and went
out of the room. He found her waking up the
three children sleeping in the hall. They sat
rubbing their eyes, their minds in a whirl of
confusion.

III

" Why have you disturbed them ? "

" I'm taking them with me. . . ."

" Shut up ! Leave them alone ! Are you mad ? " Kamala began to cry. This was too much for him ; he dragged Savitri away from the children, at which all three of them started crying. " This is a fine scene ! " he said. He thundered, " Now keep quiet. Here, Kamala, if I hear your voice I will peel the skin off your back. Babu, Sumati, lie down and shut your eyes, and shut your mouths. Sleep at once ! Obey ! "

The children fell down, put their heads on their pillows, and shut their eyes fast, a sob occasionally bursting from one or the other.

Ramani turned to Savitri and said, " Savitri, you are trying my patience. What madness is this ? Go to bed. For the last time I tell you, go to bed." He tried to take her by the hand and lead her to her bed.

" Don't touch me ! " she cried, moving away from him. " You are dirty, you are impure. Even if I burn my skin I can't cleanse myself of the impurity of your touch." He clenched his teeth and raised his hands. She said, " All right, strike me. I am not afraid." He lowered his hands and said, " Woman, get away now."

" Do you think I am going to stay here ? We are responsible for our position : we accept food, shelter, and comforts that you give, and are what we are. Do you think that I will stay in your house, breathe the air of your property, drink the water here, and eat food you buy with your money ? No, I'll starve and die in the open, under the sky, a roof for which we need be obliged to no man."

"Very well. Take your things and get out this moment."

"Things ? I don't possess anything in this world. What possession can a woman call her own except her body ? Everything else that she has is her father's, her husband's, or her son's. So take these too. . . ." She removed her diamond earrings, the diamond studs on her nose, her necklace, gold bangles and rings, and threw them at him. " Now, come on, children, get up ! Let us get out." She tried to go near the children. He barred her way. " Don't touch them or talk to them. Go yourself, if you want. They are my children." She hesitated for a moment and then said, " Yes, you are right. They are yours, absolutely. You paid the mid-wife and the nurse. You pay for their clothes and teachers. You are right. Didn't I say that a woman owns nothing ? " She broke down, staring at their fidgeting forms on the beds. " What will they do without me ? "

" They will get on splendidly without you,

don't you worry. No one is indispensable in this world."

The diamonds and the gold lay at his feet on the floor. He picked them up. " This ring and this necklace and this stud were not given by me. They are your father's."

She shrunk from them, " Take them away. They are also a man's gift."

Ramani said, " I'm very sleepy. I'm waiting to bolt the street door and go to bed ; that is, if you decide to go out."

She threw a look at the children, at him, turned round and walked out, softly closing the door behind her.

Before she reached the gate she heard the sound of the bolting of the front door. She opened the gate a little, let herself out, and saw the light in the front hall put out. " Will the children sleep there in the dark without me ? " She stood for a moment watching the light in her husband's room, and moved on when it was also put out. It was very nearly midnight. She walked down the silent street.

Chapter Seven

SHE walked all the way to the north end of the town and reached the river an hour later. Sarayu was flowing in the dark, with a subdued rumble. Summer was still a few weeks ahead, and now the water was fairly deep in some places, though in a few weeks' time the river would shrink to a thin streak of water furrowing the broiling sands.

Her mind was numb. Otherwise she could not have walked through the town at midnight. Nothing seemed to matter now, not even one's children. They were after all a husband's. . . . Couldn't she just go to the office, drag the other woman out, gash her face with her finger-nails? Wouldn't it be interesting to wait and see if he would still grovel at the feet of that slut whose face was gashed and whose hair was torn out?

Savitri sat on the last step with her feet in the dark moving water. " This is the end," she said to herself, and felt very strange. So strange indeed did this statement sound to her that she asked herself : " Am I the same old Savitri or am I someone else ? Perhaps this is just a dream. And I must be someone else posing as Savitri because I couldn't have had the courage to talk back to my husband. I have never done it in my life. I couldn't have had the courage to walk through the streets at midnight. I am afraid to go even a hundred yards from the house un-escorted ; yes, afraid, afraid of everything. One definite thing in life is Fear. Fear, from the cradle to the funeral pyre, and even beyond that, fear of torture in the other world. Afraid of a husband's displeasures, and of the dis-comforts that might be caused to him, morning to night and all night too. How many nights have I slept on the bed on one side, growing numb by the unchanged position, afraid lest any slight movement should disturb his sleep and cause him discomfort." Afraid of one's father, teachers and everybody in early life, afraid of one's husband, children, and neighbours in later life—fear, fear, in one's heart till the funeral pyre was lit, and then fear of being sentenced by Yama to be held down in a cauldron of boiling oil. . . . " How many sins have I not com-mitted ? . . . Not many, I have always per-formed my daily *pooja* without fail. I've never lied in my life, except a few uttered in child-hood. Didn't I and my sister finish off the honey in the bottle and then swear we didn't know what had happened to it ? And then that scuffle after which I said that my brother had flung the ball at the glass chimney. Poor fellow, bearing patiently all our anger and vileness and never lifting his hand on us because we were girls. What ages since I saw him, never been the same man since he married that girl from Tayur, a vicious slattern. Far away there from everybody, in Hyderabad, led about by a nose-rope like a bullock. Years since he has written a line to anyone at home ; perhaps he has forgotten all his sisters ; must have quite a dozen children by now."

Savitri felt an intense longing to see her brother and her parents. Wouldn't it be better to go round once, see everybody, and then die ? Who was so dear to one, after all, as one's parents, one's brothers and sisters, really loving and affectionate ? not a husband but one's parents—theirs was the true affection, not even one's children's. . . . Babu would perhaps not come home at all but spend his time in the office and not think of her ; Sumati and Kamala would marry and go away and get wrapped up in their own family bothers and give their mother a thought once in a way when there was nothing else to think about. . . .

" Must go and see my sister in Rangoon too. Perhaps I can see everybody, see her last, and jump into the sea while returning from Rangoon. What a happy couple those two are, never irritating each other, beautifully balanced. She has always been the luckier since childhood. She was the one to escape thrashing, to be given the first sweets and pencils, to be called up and petted by father's friends ; and no wonder the same luck persists in marriage too. Perhaps one gets the husband one deserves." She now thought of her husband. Poor man, she said ; not so bad by himself, only poisoned in mind now by that slut (was she such a heavenly creature that one should lose all one's senses ?). Hadn't he said when they talked to each other for the first time, on the fifth day of marriage, up in the lonely upstairs room, that the moment he saw her he decided to marry her, and that he would have taken his life if he hadn't got her ? How he had written to her in all the early letters that he hadn't met any-one with a skin as fair as hers, or with her eyes or hair or cheeks. She wished she had those letters with her now. She would throw them at him and say . . . The woman in the office might be really good-looking. I'm not the Savitri that I was when he wrote those letters. Give the other one, too, three children and two mis-carriages and see what she will come to ; no one except me could have retained even so much of my early looks. Day before yesterday the mirror didn't depress me. I looked quite the same as I did before my nuptials, but it was his fault, he should have come home and seen me. All the flowers and trouble absolutely wasted. Not my fault, he came only a day after I looked my best."

The Taluk office gong was being struck, and its notes came clearly through the still air. Savitri counted, one, two, three. . . . " I've never seen this hour before, always been asleep. Not always, when Babu had the chickenpox and Sumati had typhoid I've counted the gong at this hour on several nights. And also when he had his headache. How many nights have I sat up all night, yes, even at three o'clock, and held his throbbing head. Would the other one do it for an hour if he should have any pain now? Why do men have such a bad memory? He said, 'Get out, I want to sleep.'"

Three o'clock now, in an hour it would be four, then five, and six, and people would come and drag her back home or lock her up as being mad. What was the use of sitting on the river-step with a wandering mind and wasting one's time? No one who could not live by herself should be allowed to exist. " If I take the train and go to my parents, I shall feed on my father's pension; if I go back home, I shall be living on my husband's earnings, and later, on Babu. What can I do by myself?

Unfit to earn a handful of rice except by begging. If I had gone to a college and studied, I might have become a teacher or something. It was very foolish of me not to have gone on with my education. Sumati and Kamala must study up to the B.A. and not depend for their salvation on marriage. What is the difference between a prostitute and a married woman?—the prostitute changes her men, but a married woman doesn't ; that's all, but both earn their food and shelter in the same manner. Yes, Kamala and Sumati must take their University course and become independent." She laughed at herself for planning for her daughters. Who were they ? His daughters, not hers. He had said that he had paid for their coming into the world and for their upkeep here.

No one who couldn't live by herself had a right to exist. It was three, in an hour it would be four, and then five . . . people would come and drag her away.

She rose and stepped down. There was still one step, the very last submerged under water, very slippery with moss ; and then one felt the sand under one's feet ; water reached up to one's hips, and as one went further down, to one's breasts ; and now the running water tripped up one's legs from behind. She stood in the water and prayed to her God on the

Hill to protect the children. . . . " In Yama's world the cauldron must be ready for me for the sin of talking back to a husband and disobeying him, but what could I do ? What could I do . . . no, no, I can't die. I must go back home. I won't, I won't." The last sensation that she felt was a sharp sting as the water shot up her nostrils, and something took hold of her feet and toppled her over.

Chapter Eight

BURGLARY was only a side occupation for Mari. He was the locksmith, umbrella-repairer, and blacksmith of Sukkur village, which was a couple of miles from the other bank of the river. He was a burglar for various reasons; there was a predatory strain in his nature, perhaps handed down to him by his ancestors, which made him love the excitement of breaking into a house; he also valued the profits of the adventure; and he did it to please his wife. He was intensely devoted to her, and her one ambition in life was to fill a small brass pot with coins and precious metal and bury it at the root of a coconut tree which shot up from the back-yard of their little home. Tinkering at iron things gave one a steady income but a small one; and if you put up your rates you might drive your customers to the next village; if you didn't put up your rates you had an inadequate income—which made a wife unhappy and quarrelsome. Mari cared a great deal for his wife, although he chased her about and threw things at her when he was drunk.

He sallied forth once a month or so across the

river into Malgudi town, crying " Locks repaired, sirs, umbrellas repaired ! " in the
streets. During these journeys, if any locked
house caught his eye, he let himself into it at
midnight and picked up any silverware or
precious trifle that might be there.

On this day he was in town. It was a miserable day. He cried " Locks repaired, sirs, umbrellas repaired ! " till he felt as if a file were
working inside his Adam's apple, and yet his
only customer was a miser at the Market, who
wouldn't give even an anna for a new rib to his
umbrella ; he wanted it to be done for six pies.
Mari needed the six pies badly, and he did the
work ; and something else too : before handing
back the umbrella, with a deft twist of the pliers
somewhere he assured himself that it would be
crippled at the next gust of wind ; and then the
heir of a miser could thank himself for the six
pies saved !

What galled him most was that the wife at
home expected a man to return laden with
money. Time was when a man could earn at
least a rupee in the town, but nowadays it was
a mystery what people did with their broken
umbrellas. Gone were the days when locks and
keys were a luxury ; now if a key was lost
another with a lock (made in Japan) could be
bought for an anna and a half !

Mari turned his steps from the crowded Market Road, Vinayak Mudali and Grove Streets, and with a last hope moved towards Lawley Extension. Here were rich bungalows ; and people who never carried umbrellas but went about in cars. All the same occasionally there was a demand for a repairer, and payment was excellent. . . .

His voice rang through the broad silent streets of Lawley Extension. He shouted louder here than anywhere else because every house had a compound, and the message had to get through the gates and reach the people living yards away from the road. This also proved to be a profitless excursion. Mari coughed and said to himself that he might cry till he spat blood but nobody would give him a pie.

He was in the Fourth Cross Road, cursing his luck, when he saw a locked house. He slackened his pace, observed the house more fully, paced the street up and down, and went away.

He sang as he walked back to Market Road. It seemed immaterial to him if his purse contained only half an anna.

There was an old woman squatting on the narrow pavement at the Market gateway selling fried groundnut, coloured edibles, and cucumber slices, arranged on a gunny-sack spread on the ground. Mari put down his small bundle of tools and sat down before the gunny-sack.

"Get out of the way," the old woman cried.

"Ah, mother, you are really becoming blind," Mari said, moving nearer. "I am Mari."

The old woman laughed and said: "I can't see who is who at this hour. But what a nuisance the whole day, people coming and sitting down there every other minute! I am hoarse calling out. . . ." She struck a match and lit the wick peeping out of a tin container. She placed the container on an inverted basket and brightened the surroundings with the wavering flare. "I can see better now, can't I? When did you come to town, and why have you come so late, my son?"

"Have I not to earn some money before I come and spend it here? Would you give me a little pinch of anything unless I paid for it at once?"

"I am a poor wretch who has to add pie on pie; what can I do?"

"You have the cunning of a fox! You must have made a fortune by now, which you are salting and pickling somewhere, I know. Your days are nearly over, and yet your avarice has not ended; why should you not give your money to poor folk like me?" After these pleasantries Mari proceeded to business. He

125   I

bought, after much haggling, groundnut for three pies, a curved slice of cucumber for a pie, and some fried stuff for two pies, and munched them with deliberate care and attention. "A fire-like hunger inside me and this is just a pinch in some corner," he said at the end of the meal.

" Then buy some more. I have some nice things in this basket. . . ."

" You tempt me. All right, but will you take the money tomorrow ? "

" Credit day after tomorrow," the old woman said.

Mari walked over to the fountain in the Market Square, took water in his hands, and drank it. " Now it is better," he said, coming back to the old woman. " Oh, sister, give me a little tobacco and betel leaf. God will take you to Heaven for it. I have given you all my money. I have no more. I shall go raving mad if I don't get a little piece of tobacco now."

The old woman took out her greasy cloth purse, peered into it by the light of the smoky flare, picked up a piece of tobacco and a crumpled betel leaf, and flung them at Mari, grumbling, " You are the biggest scoundrel God ever made. You spend half an anna but take goods for three-quarters of an anna."

" Let me be smitten with leprosy if I have a pie more about me," said Mari, receiving the gift and putting it in his mouth. He took his tool-bag and walked away. He crossed the road, went into the spacious rest-house before the Market, and lay down in the veranda. Chewing the betel leaf and tobacco, he had a great sense of well-being ; he shut his eyes and revelled in it for some time, and fell asleep.

He got up at midnight. The Market Road was silent ; only the lights of a few late shops illuminated the road here and there. The last cinema shows were over and there was no traffic. Mari looked round ; a number of others, travellers, adventurers, and mendicants, were lying about fast asleep ; some were talking from unseen corners ; and one or two were sitting and sucking at an enchanted clay pipe filled with opium leaf, the pipe glowing in the dark.

Mari moved down the road cautiously. He abandoned the main thoroughfare at the earliest possible moment, stole along by-ways and lanes, and reached Lawley Extension.

Not for him now the broad paved roads of the Extension. Here in this locality of Government and Police officials the constables went round with thoroughness on their beats. Mari slipped into an ill-lit conservancy lane, his ears cocked to catch the creaking of police boots. When he heard footsteps he flattened himself against a wall and stood still. The policeman appeared on the edge of the road, looking down the lane, lightly breathing through his whistle, and moved away after shouting, " Stop, who are you ? Don't run, stop ! . . ."

Mari stood at the gate of the bungalow in the Fourth Cross Road, looked up and down, and vaulted over the compound wall. He closely examined the lock on the front door and squatted down so that he might not be seen from the road. He opened his tool-bag, took out a possible key, ran his file over it, and tried it on the lock. After filing it four or five times he was able to fit it into the lock. He never believed in breaking a lock open, it made things conspicuous. Opening a lock in the correct manner, and locking a house again when leaving it, was, Mari felt, a piece of courtesy which a man owed the absent householders.

Mari let himself into the house, shut the door again, and looked about by the light of a match. He was in a large furnished room. He saw a tray on a stool with betel leaves and areca-nut in it. The leaves were stiff and dry, from which Mari concluded the family must have been away for at least three days. Mari transferred the leaves and nut to his tool-bag, and examined the tray: it looked like plated nickel. He put it down—it wasn't worth the risk a man ran in carrying it about.

He opened the shelves and cupboards. Some of them were empty, and some contained only books, clothes, and other useless stuff. So these people either possessed no silver or were the sneaky sort who kept it in iron safes !

He drifted towards the *pooja* room ; there at least one could pick up odd bits of silver—tiny images of gods, incense-holders, and such things. On the way he peeped into the kitchen safe. All the vessels were empty ; only a little butter-milk, acrid and fermented, at the bottom of a vessel. He also found, wrapped in a piece of paper, a quarter loaf of bread, stiff as card-board. Mari felt happy at the sight of it ; so he needn't go away with an empty stomach. A handful of groundnut vended by that stingy hag was no food for a hungering stomach. He tried to bite the loaf of bread, but it scratched his gums and hurt the roof of his mouth ; he then soaked it in the sour buttermilk and thrust it into his mouth.

He felt contented and hoped that presently in the *pooja* room he might find at least a half-inch-high god, not worth more than a rupee and eight annas, but better than nothing, some keepsake for the wife. These householders were cunning people all the world over : if they had large images and valuable pieces for worship they took care not to leave them about, the cunning hypocrites ! Was there any true piety in a person who locked up the gods ?

At this moment a noise like that of a terraced roof crashing down came through the darkness. Mari stood stock-still, not daring even to munch his bread. And then he heard groans, and a weak voice calling someone; and again another cascade of falling bricks, groans, and further sounds of choking.

Mari realised it was none of his business to find out what it was, but to clear out immediately if he didn't want to end in jail. While moving towards the exit Mari saw a light through a window. Somebody was living in the back portion of the house. A young boy was administering medicine to an old man who was sitting up, choking and wheezing. "Never thought for a moment you were all here, friends," Mari said softly under his breath. "Your cough will burst you soon, don't worry."

He was out of the house very soon. His cheeks bulging with the dry bread, he threaded his way through dark alleys and was soon at Ellaman Street. In this part of the town a man could go about freely because the policemen slept on the pyols of houses or under the awnings of shop-fronts and got up only in the morning.

He approached the river, very much depressed. He wished he had brought away at
least the tray. Now to be going home empty-
handed after a full day out—his wife would
spit in his face if she should see what he had
brought from the town—a few withered betel
leaves. He had better not show her the leaves
but chew them off, as soon as he could take a
mouthful of water from the river and wash
down that terrible bit of bread and rid himself
of the hiccups which had been torturing him
at regular intervals all along : he had been
afraid that in the still night his hiccups might
stir up the town or awaken the policemen in
Ellaman and North Streets.

He crossed the sands towards the steps ;
swimming across here saved distance, otherwise one would have to trudge all the way to
Nallapa's Grove and cross the river. . . .

The Taluk office gong struck three. Mari
counted it and reckoned that he could be home
at four : only a few strokes across the river and
then two milestones.

Just as he reached the steps he saw, down
below at the water's edge, an apparition. He
stood petrified. Surely, this was Mohini, the
Temptress Devil, who waylaid lonely way-
farers and sucked their blood. . . . He watched
it in fascination and horror, and presently the

Mohini rose and walked into the river. " Ah, the Devil can walk on water ; at what inauspicious moment did I leave home today ? She hasn't seen me yet. I dare not move. . . ." By this time the apparition was in deep water and let out a cry : " No, no, I can't die : I must go back home. . . . " And then there was silence. Mari had by now got over his first fright, and said to himself, " The Devil can't talk, and the Devil can't drown." He ran down the steps.

He rescued Savitri before she had taken in too much water. Already the currents had carried her to the middle of the river and a little way down. Mari took hold of her hair and dragged her to the opposite bank. He rolled her over and very nearly jumped on her stomach. She opened her eyes and mumbled something.

Mari asked, " What language are you speaking ? "

She asked, " When will you be back home ? "

Mari replied, " I should have been nearly there now but for you. I am sorry I ever left the village today."

" Has Babu gone out to play ? Did he drink the coffee ? "

" I can't say. He might have. Can you get up ? "

" Is it morning ? Has the milkman come ? "

" It is nearly morning, but I can't see the milkman anywhere."

" What is the matter with him ? "

" How can I tell ? You didn't expect to find him in the river, did you ? " With this Mari shook her, rolled her, twisted her limbs. Savitri stared at the dark face bending over her and screamed, " Alas ! Somebody help me ! Thief, thief ! " Mari said to himself, " She has found me out. I am undone. This woman is uncanny," and left her and broke into a run. He cursed her as he ran : " This woman will see me in jail for my trouble. I should have let her drown herself ten times over. . . ."

Savitri awoke next morning with a throbbing head and stiff aching limbs. She realised her position now. All the old bitterness and pain revived in her. On her right, beyond the stretch of water and sand, the Town Hall tower peeped over a cluster of roofs. Savitri gazed on it and reflected that, under some roof in the cluster, *he* must be with the woman ; let him be. She must go on with her back to that cluster of roofs and never turn again towards them, never, unless he abandoned the woman and begged for pardon. She was an individual with pride and with a soul, and she wasn't going to submit to everything here-

after. Would *he* be searching for her now? It
was more likely he had brought the other one
and kept her in the house. Would she be ill-
treating the children? Savitri wished that she
had asked Janamma or Gangu to keep an eye
on the children. But . . . children? Let them
alone. They were his; he paid the midwife,
and it was his duty to look after them. Hadn't
he said that they would get on splendidly
without her? " Now what shall I do with
myself? Shall I starve to death? "

A dark hefty man and a woman appeared
before her. The woman asked, " Are you all
right now? "

" Who are you? "

" I am of Sukkur village and people call me
Ponni. My husband is a blacksmith. While he
was returning home from—never mind where
or why he had gone there, men have to go out
and work, you know—he saw you in the river
and he says that he saved your life and left you
on the bank."

" You should have left me alone," Savitri
said.

" Why do you say that? When he told me
where he had left you, I shouted to him, ' You
can't leave a woman helpless, all alone there.
Go there this minute and see if she is all right.'
But when he started someone came along to

have a wheel-band set right; when it was over and just as we were starting someone else came along with a battered lock. Oh, it is a nasty profession without any rest, but we are poor people. We can't afford to say to anyone 'Come later.' We have to live on their good-will, you know."

" You are right," Savitri said.

" I am so happy to see you alive. You are so fair, and you look rich. I can't understand how you came to be here. Why did you jump into the river ? "

" Is this your husband ? "

" Yes."

" Do you like him very much ? "

At this Ponni looked shy and smiled. Savitri said, " Suppose he took another woman and neglected you, what would you do ? "

Ponni threw a suspicious glance at her husband and asked, " Have you been up to any such trick ? "

" No, no," Mari said, and asked, turning to Savitri, " What do you mean by this, madam ?" Savitri explained to Ponni, " I don't say he has done it. Imagine for a moment . . ."

Mari asked indignantly, " Why should she imagine such a thing ? "

Savitri persisted, " If he did such a thing, what would you do ? "

Ponni said, " Let him try. Then he will know what he will get."

" But that was all that I could do," Savitri said, pointing at the river. " I have slaved for him all these years. We have children. And now he is ensnared by a—by a—by some woman. He doesn't want me."

Ponni said, " Sister, remember this. Keep the men under the rod, and they will be all right. Show them that you care for them and they will tie you up and treat you like a dog."

" What do you mean ? " Mari protested. " When have I treated you like a dog ? "

" Don't talk now," Ponni commanded. " Don't butt in when women are talking. Stay under that tree. I will call you when I want you." Mari hesitated to go. Ponni said : " Look here. It is no use your standing here. We are not going to talk to you. You have walked two stones. Rest under that tree. You will hear soon enough when you are wanted." Mari faded out of the scene. Ponni said to Savitri, " You see, that is the way to manage them. He is a splendid boy, but sometimes he goes out with bad friends, who force him to drink, and then he will come home and try to break all the pots and beat me. But when I know that he has been drinking, the moment he comes home, I trip him up from behind and push him down, and sit on his back for a little while ; he will wriggle a little, swear at me, and then sleep, and wake up in the morning quiet as a lamb. I can't believe any husband is unmanageable in this universe. . . . Sister, I can't let you sit here all day, the sun is getting warm. Where would you like to go now ? "

" Nowhere. I will stay here."

" Shall I send my husband to the town and ask him to bring your people ? "

Savitri shuddered at the suggestion.

" Or come with me to my house. My home is humble, but I will gladly clear a corner for you." Savitri declined the offer.

Ponni said, " I see you are a Brahmin and won't stay with us. I will ask someone of your own caste to receive you."

" No. Leave me alone."

" Or stay in our house. I will clear a part for you and never come there. I will buy a new pot for you, and rice, and you can cook your own food. I will never come that way. I will never cook anything in our house which may be repulsive to you. Please come with me."

" No. I won't come anywhere."

" Our village is only two stones from here. Let us walk slowly."

" Please go away. Leave me alone."

At this stubbornness Ponni lost her temper :

137

" I don't know what you are planning. You want to be neither here nor there. I don't know where you really want to go. A very fine person to deal with ! "

" Why do you trouble yourself about me ? "

" Why not ? See here, my dear lady, either you will come with me to the village or go back to the town. I won't let you stay here. If you persist in moving neither way, I will send my husband to the town and bring someone from there to carry you back home."

Savitri imagined someone coming from that cluster of roofs, tying her hand and foot, and carrying her back to the South Extension. She asked, " Which way do we go ? " in order to assure herself that it was away from the roofs and not towards them.

" I will come with you," she said, " on condition that you don't trouble me to come under your roof or any other roof. I will remain only under the sky."

Chapter Nine

RAMANI got up from bed after a night of disturbed sleep. With all his bravado before his wife, he was very much shaken by her manner. Such a thing had never happened to him at any time for fifteen years. She had always been docile and obedient, and the fire inside her was a revelation to him now. Though he had invited her to walk out of the house last night, he had not expected her to do it. He had expected she would go into the dark room and sulk for a few days, a few days more than usual ; then she was bound to come to her senses and accept things as they were. He felt irritated when people made any fuss. A man had a right to a little fun now and then, provided it didn't affect his conduct at home. No doubt it took him home rather late, but that could have been rectified by a little persistent persuasion on her part ; all this sullenness and dictation was not the right way to set about it ; he expected to be coaxed and requested ; he told himself that people could get anything from him if only they knew the proper way of approaching him. It would be a very bold person indeed who tried to dictate to him.

He had never tolerated any advice from anyone —not even from his father, who, a few years before his death, when Ramani passed his Matriculation, had advised him to continue his studies and was told, " I know better what I must do."

Ramani was self-made. He hadn't waited for anybody's help or advice. If he had waited for other people to tell him what to do he might have earned a B.A. and become now a clerk in an office or a lawyer with a miserable practice. As it was, through his own, very own, effort and enterprise he was making a clear five hundred a month, in salary alone, and persons with double or treble degrees constantly applied to him for jobs worth fifty or sixty under him ! (This last gave him a certain compensating satisfaction at being without a University degree. He sometimes regretted it because he had often seen B.A.s giving themselves airs, though they could not earn a hundred rupees a year, the ridiculous beings ! He occasionally longed for a degree simply in order that he might snub the graduates a little more thoroughly, on their own ground.)

He was entirely self-made, and that proved one was right and needed no advice from others, and least at all from a wife. Of course, he granted, there was some sense in the Women's

Movement : let them by all means read English
novels, play tennis, have their All-India Conference, and go to pictures occasionally ; but
that should not blind them to their primary
duties of being wives and mothers ; they
mustn't attempt to ape the Western women, all
of whom, according to Ramani's belief, lived in
a chaos of promiscuity and divorce. He held
that India owed its spiritual eminence to the
fact that the people here realised that a woman's
primary duty (also a divine privilege) was being
a wife and a mother, and what woman retained the right of being called a wife who dis-
obeyed her husband ? Didn't all the ancient
epics and Scriptures enjoin upon woman the
strictest identification with her husband ? He
remembered all the heroines of the epics whose
one dominant quality was a blind stubborn
following of their husbands, like the shadow
following the substance.

" Will you promise not to go near her
again ? " and what else ? " You are not
having me and her at the same time." A
fine way to talk to a husband. Threatened to
walk out like a servant. All the kindness and
consideration entirely wasted. How could she
forget the six-sovereign necklace he had bought
for her at the beginning of his career, when he
had not a bank account and was subsisting

on insurance canvassing? How could she forget the misery and anxiety he suffered when she had labour pains and the rest? Like a servant threatening to leave, unless something or other was done! No one had any right to object to his friendship with Shanta Bai—that splendid creature with her understanding heart and cultured outlook. Savitri ought not to behave as if her husband was like some low-class fellow who kept a mistress. . . .

He was decidedly not going to worry about her or search for her. She had walked out of her own will; she would have to face the consequences, of course; old enough to know what she was doing. Firmness was everything in life; that was the secret of success with women. If they found a man squeamish they would drive him about with a whip. He was certain she would return and apologise when her madness passed. This was only a different version of the sulking in the dark room. She might now be sulking in a dark corner of some friend's house. After all, where could she go? He was going to show that *he* wasn't the loser anyway.

In the morning the children sat up rather dazed. They were bewildered and unhappy. They huddled together in a corner of the hall. Sumati took upon herself the task of playing the mother. She went to the cook and said, " You must give us coffee."

" Where is your mother ? " asked the cook.

Sumati, not being able to answer, said "Wait a moment," and came to the hall to consult her brother. " Babu, the cook asks where is Mother. What shall I tell him ? "

" What will you tell him ? "

" I don't know."

" Tell him that it is none of his business."

Kamala said, " Perhaps he knows where she is : he might have seen her somewhere last night," and burst into tears.

Ramani came that way. He now felt that all the responsibility of running the household had descended on him. He was going to prove that no one was indispensable in this world. He also felt that this was his opportunity to introduce certain reforms and economies which he had been suggesting for years to a deaf wife. (He was going to abolish the cooking of brinjals in the house, tell the cook to stay at night, have tea instead of coffee in the afternoons, cut the milk bill by half, and so on.)

He pinched Kamala's cheeks, rumpled Babu's hair, and patted Sumati's back. Decidedly, he was going to make them happy. They were not to miss their mother. " Have you all had your coffee ? " he asked with his brightest smile. His unusual affability comforted the children. " Now, babies," he said, " come to my room."

" All of us ? " Babu asked, surprised. Admission to Father's room was a rare privilege, and only Kamala had it occasionally.

He seated them in a row on the floor, squatted before them like a village schoolmaster, and worked himself up to his best canvassing technique—a gift which made him net a lakh's worth of policies a year in the early days. " Now, babies, you must not be miserable because your mother is not here."

" Where is she ? " Kamala asked.

" She has only gone to Talapur. Her father was suddenly taken ill. I had a telegram from Talapur at my office yesterday."

The children listened to this story without enthusiasm, and Ramani asked, " Why are you all silent ? " Babu, being the eldest, believed the story the least. He wanted to ask several questions : why she had gone at midnight, why she had removed the jewels before going, why there had been so much of argument and tears ; but he dared not put questions to his father. Kamala asked, " Why didn't anyone go with her to the station ? "

" There was no one to go with her. I couldn't, because you were all alone here."

Sumati asked, " Was a carriage brought to take her to the station ? "

" Yes. It was waiting in the street."

" But we didn't see it."

" I thought, Father," Kamala ventured, " that you and Mother had a big quarrel because she cried so much when she went out."

Ramani said, " She wanted to take you all with her. I said ' No.' She became cross. You have school, you know."

" Why did she cry so much, Father ? "

" Her father was very ill. Wouldn't you cry very much if I should be very ill ? " He looked at Babu and said, " Why are you blinking ? Do you want to ask anything ? "

Babu felt obliged to ask, " When will Mother be back ? "

Ramani replied that it would depend on her father's health. " Have you all bathed ? "

" It is very difficult to make Kamala bathe," said Sumati. " Every day Mother had such a bother to make her bathe ! "

Ramani looked at Kamala and said, " No, no. You aren't like that, are you ? You are a nice girl. Sumati will give you a bath. Now, will you be a nice little girl ? "

" Yes, Father."

Ramani changed his mind. " Sumati, I

think you had better leave her alone. She will bathe herself. Kamala, you are five years old ; you must become self-reliant."

" Yes, Father."

Just when the children were starting for school he said, " What do you do for tiffin ? " The girls told him that they came home in the afternoons. Ramani said : " I will tell the cook to stay. Come in the afternoon and see that he serves you properly. You must all learn to attend to your affairs yourselves. Self-reliance is the first thing you must learn in life. Do you also come home in the afternoon, Babu ? "

" No, Father, I come home only in the evening."

" Do you mean to tell me that you starve till the evening ? It won't do." What did she mean by letting Babu starve till the evening ? " You must carry a small tiffin packet for the afternoon, Babu." Babu felt his father's attentions irksome. To him there was something shameful and degrading in carrying a packet and eating it in the school. His mother had given up the attempt as hopeless. Now Father was suggesting it. Why could not Father leave people alone ?

" I will manage somehow today," Babu said.

" What will you do ? You can't starve," said

Ramani, and called the cook and told him, " Make a tiffin packet for Babu."

" The tiffin is not ready yet," said the cook.

Ramani scowled at the cook. " What do you mean by it ? Don't you know that this boy is to have something for the afternoon ? Wonderful work you are doing, to be sure. Let me not catch you at this sort of thing again. As soon as you prepare the tiffin, make a packet of it and take it to his school." Babu was horrified at the prospect. His schoolfellows would surely stand round and grin at him and his cook as he swallowed the tiffin. It was simply not done. He protested mildly, but Father would not hear of it. " I know what is best for you. Don't contradict your elders." Babu accepted his fate with gloomy resignation. It was no use arguing with Father. Life was becoming messy and rotten. " Now you may all go. Wait for me in the evening. I will take you all to a cinema."

Sumati and Kamala clapped their hands in joy, but Babu asked, " In the evening ? "

" Yes, sir."

" I have to play cricket, Father."

" Not when your father wants you to go to the pictures with him."

" We are playing against the Y.M.U. next week, and our captain will be very angry if I miss practice."

" Look here, Babu, you are a very——" He was irritated and was about to begin a long analysis of Babu's character, but he checked himself as he remembered that he had to be very kind to the children. " You must learn to be a nice boy, Babu. You must think of your sisters. They can't enjoy a picture without your company, can they ? Don't refuse them that pleasure. You must also think of others ; you must not be selfish."

" I like pictures, Father, but I have to practise for a match. I said——"

" Well, well, well ! Don't go on saying the same thing over and over again. Your match can wait." Before going to the office he called the cook and told him, " Make tea for everybody in the afternoon. Coffee only in the mornings."

§

Ramani left the office at five o'clock in the evening. On the way he stopped before a restaurant and bought some sweets. The moment he came home he asked if they had all had their afternoon curd and rice and tiffin and tea correctly, and particularly if Babu had his tiffin at school. Kamala said, " I don't like the smell of tea, and so I drank only half a tumbler."

148

"No, that won't do. You must learn to like tea. It is a very good drink."

"All right, Father. From tomorrow I will try to like tea."

Ramani was greatly pleased. He had not known till now that his children were so manageable. "Did you like your tea, Sumati?" he asked, turning to the other. She said "Yes," and added that it didn't make any difference to her whether it was tea or coffee.

He gave the packet of sweets to Sumati and said, "Share it among yourselves."

He had bought rather a large quantity of the sweets, and so, though the children started enthusiastically, they couldn't eat more than half of what they took. Ramani shook his head disapprovingly: "You mustn't get into the habit of wasting things. Babu, you have left the largest quantity; that won't do. You are a sportsman. You must eat a lot and grow strong. Polish it off, otherwise I will never call you a cricket player. Go on." Babu had been the first to arrive at the stage of retching, but now he grabbed the stuff on the plate, gulped it down, and looked at his father for approval. "Great boy," Ramani said. "You will be in the India Eleven some day." Babu was tremendously pleased though the sweets turned in his stomach.

He took them to the Palace Talkies, which

was showing a Laurel and Hardy film. The children sat completely absorbed. They forgot this world, its troubles, and the absence of a mother, while they watched the antics of the comedians.

Ramani got up in the middle of the show, whispering to them : " Stay here till I come back and pick you up. Don't leave the theatre even if I am delayed a bit."

" I will look after them," Babu said.

" Father, what shall we do if somebody comes and orders us out of the theatre ? " Kamala asked.

§

" Life is one continuous boredom," Shanta Bai said, locking her arms behind her head and leaning back on the pillow. " I started out in life wanting to do things, but here I am vegetating. All day long I listen to Pereira's humour and to Kantaiengar's rudeness, and then come here and lie down on the couch. ' As wind along the waste——' Have you read Omar Khayyám ? "

" Who is he ? " Shanta Bai's literary allusions distressed him.

" The Persian poet."

" I don't know the Mahommedan language," Ramani said innocently, and Shanta Bai began to lecture him on Omar Khayyám and Fitz-Gerald.

"I can't exist without a copy of *The Rubá'iyát* ; you will always find it under my pillow or in my bag. His philosophy appeals to me. Dead yesterday and unborn tomorrow. ' What, without asking whither hurried hence ' and so on. The cup of life must be filled to the brim and drained ; another and another cup to drown the impertinence of this memory. In this world Khayyám is the only person who would have understood the secret of my soul. No one tries to understand me ; that is the tragedy of my life. Khayyám says : Into this Universe and why not knowing, etcetera. I am as wind along the waste."

Ramani went over to the edge of her cot, sat down there, and tried to hold her hands. Shanta Bai took away her hands and pleaded : " Please leave me alone. I am in no mood now."

" Are you sure ? "

" Absolutely. You may sit here if you like, but please don't touch me."

Ramani folded his arms across his chest. Shanta Bai hummed a little tune to herself and said, tossing her head, " I am so unhappy that I have not brought my violin with me. I am in a mood to play."

" What a pity that I didn't know it ! "

" Have you a violin at home ? "

" No. I would have bought one for you."

" Oh, you are so good to me. I don't know how I am ever going to repay your kindness."

Ramani's heart thrilled at these words. " I have told you not to talk of repayment. When I know I like a person, I like the person, that is all, and I will do anything for the person. Please don't talk of repayment on any account."

Presently she said, " Pereira told me that there is a Laurel and Hardy comic at the Palace. Shall we go there tonight ? "

" I am so sorry, not tonight. I have to be with my children. My wife has gone to her parents."

" Oh," Shanta Bai said with resignation. " H'm, just my luck, that is all. I would have so loved a picture tonight ! Just my luck, that is all."

" Don't mistake me, dear," Ramani begged.

" Not at all. Your family duties first. I was only cursing my luck." She dismissed the pictures with a sigh. She hummed a few tunes and Ramani said that she sang divinely. She said, " Would you mind putting out the light ? I feel that darkness would be more soothing to my soul now. . . . I do so hate these electric bulbs. . . ."

Ramani put out the light.

The Taluk office gong struck nine. Ramani counted it and jumped up, muttering : " Goodness ! I never thought it was nine. The children will be waiting : the poor things must be very hungry and sleepy."

Chapter Ten

As soon as they entered the village Savitri asked, " Have we arrived ? "

" Yes."

" I will stay here. You may go to your house."

" Here ? On the roadside ? You are not talking sensibly, if you will forgive me for saying so."

" There is nothing wrong in it. Or I will go over to that field and stay there."

" And get bitten by a cobra ? You can't stay anywhere in the open. You are not the kind of person who ought to risk it. You will gather a crowd round you, and you will be suffocated by the crowd if nothing worse happens. Don't be foolish, madam. Come with me to our house and stay there just for this day. We will see if anything is possible tomorrow. God is great. He will show us a way."

Savitri allowed herself to be taken to the house. She was too dazed and faint to persist.

Sukkur village consisted of about a hundred houses and six streets. Around the village there were immense stretches of paddy fields. Ponni lived in a hovel, with an extension of thatched shed abutting the crooked street, which served as Mari's workshop.

By this time they had gathered a small crowd of shepherds, urchins, and idlers behind them. People came out of their houses and stared at Savitri. One or two shouted to Ponni, " Who is this lady ? " Ponni passed on without replying.

Ponni said, as soon as they reached her house, " You come from the town. Perhaps you live in a palatial house there. I don't know if you will find my hut tolerable." Mari had come running in advance and opened the door. He hurriedly pushed away odds and ends and metal junk, which cluttered their small window-less front room. Ponni entered the house, picked up a broom, and swept the floor. She took out her best mat (which had a coloured pattern of a Japanese girl holding an umbrella), unrolled it, and requested Savitri to sit down on it. Savitri declined the mat and sat on the floor. Ponni said, " That is what I don't like about you, madam." She turned to her husband and said, " Come with me." Mari followed her. They stood in the back-yard where a tall coconut tree shot up into the sky. She asked : " Have you any money ? None, of course, I know."

" What could I do ? "

" You will see me in the streets before we have done with each other," she said. " Here is the lady. We shall have to give her something that she will accept from us. How do you propose to get it ? " Mari blinked desperately and looked away. She said, " Now get up this tree and pluck a couple of coconuts. We will beg her to drink at least the water in them." Mari hugged the tree and pulled himself up. " Mind you don't throw them on the tiles. Keep them ready. I will be back soon," she said, and went out. She hurried down the street and went to a shop where a miscellany of goods were sold. Ranganna, the shopman, was squatting amidst his articles. He asked, " What can I give you, good woman ? "

" I hope I see you well. How are your children ? "

" They are quite well."

" Is your wife all right now ? "

" Yes, yes, as well as she could be ; that is all I can say. What can I give you ? "

" If you have plantains, please give me the four ripest ones."

" With pleasure," said the shopman, and held his hand for the money.

Ponni looked hurt. " Why should you be so suspicious? Will I run away with your money?"

" Did I say so ? I was just wondering if the fruits were ripe enough for you."

" I will see for myself," said Ponni, and hopped up a platform before the shop. She pulled up a bunch of plantains which was hanging by a string. " These are excellent," she said. She selected four, plucked them out, and jumped down the platform. She asked, " How much ? "

" Eight pies," said the shopman.

" Too dear, too dear," said Ponni, shaking her head disapprovingly. " How many fruits do you want at a quarter of an anna for six ? I will give you four pies, or, say, five pies for your sake. I will bring the money tomorrow."

" I can't give you anything on credit," said the shopman ; but Ponni was off. " I don't know what to do with this frightful woman," said the shopman.

Ponni set the coconut and the plantains before Savitri. Savitri said, " I don't need these."

" Only fruits and coconut. I knew that you wouldn't take anything else touched by me, so I have brought only fruits and coconut."

" I am not hungry," Savitri said.

Ponni persisted and argued, and there was no escape. And so Savitri had to confess, though she felt very awkward while doing it, " I am resolved never to accept food or shelter which I have not earned."

" A nice thing you are saying, my lady ! What can you do, with your soft hands ? I should be dragged to hell if I made you do any work for me. . . ."

" It is a foolish thing to say. If you don't want me to starve, give me some work. I can cook, scrub, sew. I know a little gardening too. I had a beautiful garden once. I can look after children. Have you no children ? "

" Ah, cursed me ! We have been married for twenty years and I have promised offerings to all our gods, but I am not blessed yet."

" What a pity ! I have three children. My son is just thirteen. He is very intelligent and knows a lot of things about electricity. My two girls are reading in a school ; very intelligent creatures."

" You are a blessed being, my lady. God will protect you. The difficulty that has risen before you like a mountain will soon vanish like the dew. . . . Please take this coconut, sister. It rends my heart to see you starve. You have been in the water a long time."

" I am not hungry," Savitri said.

§

Ponni sought her husband out in his work-shop. He had just done a little riveting job on a barrow and was arguing his terms with some heat. Ponni called him aside and asked, " Do you want a halter round your neck ? "

" No."

" Then do something about that lady in there. She has been starving since the morning, and if she dies the police will come on you for murder ; and they will be right because you are going about as if she were none of your business but only mine. You were the person who found her, remember."

" She is a lady, and so I thought I needn't come to that side."

" Ah, a virtuous man indeed ! You wouldn't speak to a lady, would you ? Find out something for that lady to do so that she may take her food and live."

" Let her come and work these bellows. It will be a good piece of work."

" Wouldn't you like it ? A fine high-caste lady to touch these worm-eaten bellows ! Think of something else before I come again." She turned to go. She added, " If she dies I will tell the police that you killed her, and they will believe it, be sure."

When she was gone Mari beat his brow and said to his customer, " I sometimes think that it would be better to let the police take me and hang me than be married to that woman."

" Why should the police hang you ? "

" There is a mad woman in there who won't touch food unless she is given work. Hard enough for men to get work in these days."

" What sort of woman is she ? "

" Go and see her for yourself."

The customer went in and saw Savitri. He came out and remarked, " She is an eyeful. Won't somebody marry her ? Or I will give her money." And he made a ribald suggestion.

Mari, after disposing of the customer, went in and told his wife, " I will go and see if there is anything for this lady, but what are the things she can do ? "

" She can cook, sew, and scrub. What more does a woman need to know? She also says that she knows a little gardening."

Mari went out.

§

He left the house briskly enough, but as soon as he came to the street he stopped, not having the faintest idea of what he should do. He didn't know how anyone set about getting a job, much less how a woman did it. He had inherited his foundry from his father, and had never applied to anyone for work ; and now to go and beg for the sake of that woman. . . . He resented the idea. For a moment he reflected how free he would have been now if he had let her float down the river : if her fate was good she would have survived it somehow, and if she had been destined to die she would have died in spite of any rescue, and he told himself that he would not have been particularly responsible for her death if he had left her alone. He felt angry with his wife for her fussing. Why couldn't she leave the woman alone ? If she didn't want food it was entirely her business. This was what came of allowing too much liberty to women ; they ought to be kept under proper control and then all would be well. He felt irritated with himself at his own helplessness before his wife. . . .

" Did you start out only to stand in the street and meditate ? " asked Ponni, peeping out of the house. Mari moved down the road without turning his head. "You have started walking. Where do you intend to go ? " she asked.

" You can leave it to me, and go in," he shouted back, and felt a great relief at having said something of his own after all. He went down the street and stopped before Ranganna's shop. He occasionally enjoyed sitting on the platform before the shop and chatting with Ranganna and his customers ; he had also a hope now that Ranganna might be able to suggest something.

Ranganna received Mari coldly. Mari did not notice it, but moved on to his favourite seat on the platform, and said, " Well, well, well, how are you, brother ? "

" If you let your wife come this way again I will call the police," said Ranganna.

" That is a big word you are uttering. What has she done ? "

" You already owe me an anna, which I don't know when you are going to pay. And that woman walks in as if she owned the shop. . . ."

Mari saw that it was no time for companionship. He rose to his feet, saying : " You talk too much. I fear you may suffer from sore throat tonight. You have not the guts to stop a woman from snatching a thing in your shop. Why do you come and complain to me ? "

He crossed some of the lanes and cross-paths and went into the Brahmin street. She was a Brahmin lady and somebody might take her in. He stood at the beginning of the street, re-flectively looking at the houses, wondering who was most likely to be useful to him. There was the big landlord in whose house Ponni had, during certain seasons, done odd jobs ; there was the teacher with whom Mari was familiar, having repaired the pulley over his well a number of times and soldered a leaky pot an equal number of times ; then there was the other landlord, the young man with a violent temper; and his brother-in-law in the opposite house ; and the police inspector ; and the man who had married the big landlord's second daughter ; and then the village accountant.

He drew blank here. In the big landlord's house they wouldn't have anything to do with an adventuress, the teacher was too poor to burden himself with a guest or a servant, the young landlord was tight-fisted, and on the threshold of the police inspector's house Mari changed his mind. " Keep out of his way," his instinct told him.

Mari tramped the village streets up and down, spoke to all sorts of people about the woman, but received no help from anyone. Everyone was interested, curious, and even excited. They offered to go to his house and have a look at her, but none could give her work, though all offered her their charity.

Mari started back home, completely depressed. He resolved to suggest once again bellows-blowing for the lady. While passing before the old village temple, he stopped and fervently prayed for a way out. And an idea flashed on him.

The priest of the temple lived in the same street. The old man was sitting on the pyol of his house with a couple of his grandchildren playing about him. Mari stood before him and said, " My salutations to you, my noble master."

" Who are you ? " asked the old man, half closing his eyes in his effort to catch the identity of his visitor.

" I am Mari, my master, your humble slave."

" Mari, you are a vile hypocrite," said the old man.

" What sin have I committed to deserve these harsh words ? "

" I sent my boy thrice to your place, and thrice have you postponed and lied. It was after all for a petty, insignificant repair that I sent for you."

" Nobody came and called me, master. I swear I would have dropped everything and come running if only the lightest whisper had reached me. Whom did you send ? "

" Why should I send anyone ? After all, some petty repair—I thought I might have a word with you about it if you came to the temple ; but you are a godless creature ; no wonder your wife is barren. How can you hope to prosper without the grace of Muruga ? "

" Yours are words of wisdom. I promise that hereafter I will come to the temple twice a week and bring him a coconut once a month. Now, here I am awaiting your command."

The old man was appeased by this submission

and said, " It is not ten minutes' work for a workman like you. Wait a minute."

" I obey your command," said Mari.

The old man got down from the pyol, looked at Mari, shading his eyes with his webbed, shrunken hands, and said, " You don't look too well, not a quarter of what you were before." It was only in the old man's eyes that Mari looked pulled down, but, for the sake of politeness, Mari felt obliged to agree. " I too am growing old. All kinds of ills and bothers. . . ."

The old man went in and returned half an hour later carrying three old umbrellas in his hands ; behind him followed a youngster— employed in the house for cleaning the cow-shed—carrying on his head a basket filled with junk. With difficulty the old man unfurled the umbrellas, and said : " These are practically new, will be good enough to use for another ten years, if only a little rib or two is fixed up. I have been telling the boys to take these to you for ages, and they have all been postponing and lying. Everyone is a vile hypocrite."

" I will make these brand-new," Mari said. He examined them, reflecting gloomily on the hours he would have to spend over these wretched things ; and the old man was a miser.

The old man took out of the basket a bunch

of grappling-hooks, four brass locks, a zinc bucket, and a blunt scythe, all of which needed very badly Mari's healing touch. Mari reflected, " Two days of profitless labour," and said, " I will make these brand-new for you, master."

" What will you charge me for the whole lot ? "

" I will take anything you give. What I value most is your blessing."

" How long will you take to repair these ? "

" Three days, master."

" Can't you do it in a day ? "

" I will try," said Mari, and then opened the subject. " Would you not like somebody to sweep the gods' shrine, scrub it, and tend the garden ? "

" No," said the old man. " What am I here for ? "

" Ah," began Mari, his wit sharpened by desperation, " you have nobler work to do, my master," and told him about Savitri.

" What have you to do with her ? " asked the old man.

" Nothing, master, except that I have given her shelter in our humble home."

" Why have you done it ? "

" How can I say ? Fate thrusts such troubles on us at times."

" What do you care for her ? "

"I really don't. My wife has taken a liking to her. It is really her doing, and she won't let me rest till I find some work for this woman."

"If she won't let you rest, thrash her ; that is the way to keep women sane. In these days you fellows are impotent mugs, and let your women ride you about." After this homily the old man said, "I won't have any woman in the temple. She will start some mischief or other and then the temple will get a bad name." Mari took upon himself the task of assuring the old man of Savitri's character, but the old man would not accept it. "There must be something wrong about her if she has no home and has to seek a livelihood outside ; her husband must have driven her out. Why will a husband drive a wife out ? "

"I know some sorrow has brought her out of her home," said Mari. He had told everyone that Savitri had been found wandering on the outskirts of the village ; he had not told anyone how she had really been found, fearing that it might lead to questions about his nocturnal movements. "She is resolved to work and earn. It has grown in her as a madness. She has been starving and won't touch even fruit. I am afraid she may die in our house."

"Drive her out and don't worry about her," said the old man.

167

Mari felt desperate. He felt that it might be useful to remind the other of his debt. He said, " I will repair these things in a day, and do any other work you may want me to do, but please let this woman work in your temple."

" The iron bands around our grain-barrel are rather loose. Will you fix them up ? "

" Yes, master, and you needn't give me an anna for all the work. Only, please employ this woman."

" I am not unwilling to have a servant, but where am I to find the money to pay her ? You fellows nowadays don't bring offerings to the god. In the days of your fathers and grand-fathers I could have engaged ten such servants for the temple. Nowadays you fellows want to worship the god free ; no offerings, not even a piece of coconut."

Mari promised to mend his irreligious ways and also undertook to reform some of his friends, and said, " She won't demand much. Just give her something to live on, and she will be contented. Even rice will do, but please engage her. I will always be grateful to you for this kindness." He significantly lifted the grap-pling-hooks and said, " A little welding may also be necessary for this." He then looked at the umbrellas fixedly.

The priest said, " If I give her a half measure

of rice and a quarter of an anna a day, will she be prepared to accept it and work ? "

" I think she will, master."

" If so, bring her here. I will have a look at her. If I don't see anything wrong—people can't deceive me, I can measure anyone at a glance—I will engage her. But not a grain more than a half measure."

§

Ponni said to Savitri : " My husband has found some work for you. I don't know if you will like it. I am sure if he had used his intelligence a little more he could have found a better job for you."

Mari said fervently, " I swear by all our gods that nothing better could be found. I searched everywhere and asked everyone."

" Who are you to say what is good enough for this lady ? "

" I never said any such thing. I saw everyone from the Headman down."

" Do you mean to imply that what you have found is the best for the lady ? "

Savitri cut into the middle of this discussion : " Any work which will keep my life in my body, though why it should I can't say, is suitable for me. I don't want to depend on anyone hereafter for the miserable handful of food I need every day."

"You say hard words, my lady. May God grant that the sorrow which has risen before you like a mountain may soon vanish like the dew! May the God on the Hill dispel the pain in your soul!" With this prelude she told Savitri what work her husband had found for her.

Savitri felt very happy. She saw a new life opening before her. What more fitting life, she thought, could one choose than serving a god in his shrine? A half measure of rice was more than what she deserved, she felt. She could manage very well with it. She would dedicate her life to the service of God, numb her senses and memory, forget the world, and spend the rest of her years thus and die. No husband, home, or children. Ah, children! She would harden herself not to yearn for them. She would pray for them at the shrine night and day, and God would protect them : they could grow, go their ways, and tackle life according as fate had ordained for each of them. What was this foolish yearning for children, this dragging attachment? One ought to do one's duty and then drift away. Did the birds and the animals worry about their young ones after they had learnt to move? Why should she alone think of them night and day? Babu, Sumati, and Kamala were quite grown-up now; but Kamala gave no end of trouble over bath and food. Suppose she grew dirty and emaciated? Savitri dismissed this fear with a desperate effort. They were his children. He had paid for the midwife and for clothes, and for everything. He had said that she had no right to wake them up. Into this jumble of reflections Ponni intruded with, " Madam, don't you like this work ? "

" I do. I do like it very much. When shall we go there ? "

" Tomorrow morning. It is late now. . . . I beg of you not to fast any longer. Please eat at least two of these plantains and drink a little of the coconut water. Please rest here tonight. You will be making me very proud and happy if you will kindly accept my hospitality for just this night. You can go away tomorrow morning." Ponni's eyes glistened with tears as she made this request. She added, " I will prostrate myself at your feet and never rise unless you say ' Yes.' "

Savitri said, " All right. I will take something."

Eating food that was her own had grown into a perfect obsession, and so she needed some excuse for accepting the plantains and the coconut. She comforted her conscience by saying that this was the very last time in her life she would be doing it, and that it was her duty to show a little more regard for Ponni's feelings. She mentioned her hunger as the least urgent of the reasons.

§

Next morning Mari and his wife escorted Savitri to the priest's house. Savitri went through it all as if in a trance, unconvinced of the reality of things. How could the one now tramping a village street with unknown people, in search of employment, like a boy just out of college, be the old Savitri of South Extension, wife of So-and-so? Gangu, her old friend, could not have done a thing like this !

They stood before the priest's house. Mari shouted, " Oh, master, master ! " A little boy came to the street and said, " Grandpa is at his prayers and asks you not to shout."

After some time the old man came out, wrapped in a deep-red shawl. He went to the pyol and sat on it, muttering : " Couldn't you wait till I finished my prayers ? No chance for a man to meditate in this world with black-guards like you about. Why couldn't you have come a little later ? Hm, let bygones be bygones. You are of course come about that woman. Am I right ? "

" Absolutely right, my master, that is what I have come about."

The old man laughed, rather pleased with himself at guessing Mari's mission so correctly. He shaded his eyes, looked at Ponni, and asked, " Is this the woman ? " And added, " What is the matter with you, madam, that you should run away from home ? "

" This is my wife, Ponni ; she is not the one who wants to work. She has merely accompanied the other lady. This is the lady." He whispered to Savitri, " Please move a little to this side, madam, so that he may see you properly." Savitri shifted her position, feeling awkward at having to exhibit herself. The old man said : " What is the use of coming all the way if you keep yourself invisible ? Come nearer. Let us have a look at you. I never decide without looking at a person, and no one can deceive me. I can measure a person at a glance, understand ? Come nearer." Savitri blushed, hung down her head, and felt very uneasy at having to display herself, with the sun's rays illuminating her on one side. . . .

The old man looked at her and said he was surprised that a person like her was wandering in the world unattached. He put to her a number of questions which Savitri could not answer. When she opened her lips once or twice to say something, she found herself trembling and unable to say a word. Ponni intervened and said, " Why should you ask these questions ? There are wounds which must not be prodded." Mari tried to check her. He whispered, " Keep quiet. You will be irritating him." To which she replied aloud, " You can keep quiet if you like. I will talk to my master." She asked the old man, " Will you be offended if I talk to you ? "

" Who are you ? Oh, you are . . . I know. Why should I be offended ? Anybody may talk to me. I am a servant of God. I am an old man."

Saying this made him lose the thread of his previous talk with Savitri. Ponni said abruptly, " Master, I am like a granddaughter to you, and I will talk to you freely. God has not blessed me with an artful tongue. I utter what I have in my soul."

" True, true. One must utter the strictest truth," said the old man.

" So will I. I want to ask you plainly whether you are going to engage this lady or not."

" I am not," said the old man promptly.

" All right, we will go home. Come on," said Ponni. Savitri felt dejected. So back again to the life of charity and dependence. Mari apologised to the old man : " Please don't be offended. She doesn't mean it."

" I do mean it," said Ponni. " You promise one thing and do another. You are not fortunate enough to have a lady like this in your temple, that is all. And I will tell you another thing : send someone to fetch all the broken umbrellas and rubbish you have sent for repairs. If you don't send someone immediately I will throw it all into the manure dump. . . ."

The mention of the old umbrellas had a good effect. The old man said, " Woman, you are too impatient. Who said that this person would not be engaged ? "

" You. Why do you ask things that are painful ? "

" Just to know if I am dealing with the right person."

" That is not the way, my master. I need not tell you, master, because you are learned and wise, whereas I am a stupid woman. You can see her, and take her in good trust and on our word, and if you find anything wrong with her later, you can dismiss her. There are questions which hurt one, you mustn't ask them."

" I only want to know why she has run away from home. Without knowing it, how can I have her in the temple ? If its reputation suffers . . ." Savitri shuddered at the implication of this remark.

Ponni said, " There are a hundred reasons

175

for a person to leave home. If this man by my side tries any new tricks I will walk out of home, and that will be the last he will see of me, and people who ask why and what, how and when, will get the proper reply from me. You want us to do all sorts of things for you. Why should we do it? Just for the sake of friendship. And yet you won't do us a little good turn for the same friendship."

"I never said I wouldn't do it, my good woman."

"Will you engage this lady or not? That is what I want to know."

"Of course I will. I am getting old. I really want somebody to keep the temple tidy."

§

The temple had been built fifty years before by a local philanthropist, and dedicated to Subramanya, the peacock-enthroned god, the young son of Shiva. It was a small structure of brick and mortar, the inner shrine surmounted by a carved turret, now discoloured by time and weather, with an open circular corridor running between the shrine and the high outer wall.

Savitri and her friends waited in the street while the old man fumbled with a bunch of keys and opened the tall doors at the temple portal. Over it stood a mossy, dun-coloured peacock which once upon a time must have been as white as the plaster it was made of. The priest pushed the doors with his chest; they parted with a groan.

" Come in. Don't try to spend the whole day standing there," the old man said, and walked in.

" Have you no kinder words to say, sir?" Ponni retorted.

" Hush ! " Mari said, " he doesn't mean any harm. You will irritate him if you speak like this."

Ponni turned on her husband with a hiss. " Go away and mind your own business, do you understand? We can look after ourselves quite well without you." Mari hesitated. Ponni cried, " Now begone ! Go and open your tool-shed and earn some money. There may be people waiting for you. Don't waste the morning gaping at us. We can look after ourselves quite well."

" Can't I wait till the shrine is opened, so that I may prostrate myself at God's feet before I begin the day's work ? "

" All right. Sit down there. Don't follow us about with your remarks. Sit down there and wait till the shrine is opened and then disappear. I hope you understand simple words."

Mari grunted something and sat down at the portal. Ponni said, " It is no use losing one's temper." And to Savitri, " Come on, madam. Don't mind him ; he doesn't know how to behave when there are respectable people about." The priest had gone round the corridor once and was back again at the starting-point. He was furious. " Do you want me to be telling you ' Come on, come on ' at every step ? I go round thinking you are following me, and talking, and you are still here ! "

" It will cost nothing to repeat your words to us again."

" Here ? " asked the old man, horrified. " What can I tell you here ? I was going round showing you where you have to do what, and you are content to stay behind. You people will kill me one day, making me walk round and round this corridor till I am dizzy. I am not in the prime of life now. Keep it in mind." He hobbled along, tapping his staff on the cobbled pavement. Savitri and Ponni followed him. He pointed at various corners saying, " This is where you will have to do a little tidying." He stopped at almost every bit of litter, saying, " This must not be here, do you understand ? This is what you will get paid for." When they came to the portion of the corridor that was overshadowed by the branches of an immense mango tree growing in the field outside, he spent nearly half an hour pointing at every leaf which the tree had shed down. " I have asked those rascals to do something about their tree and they won't do it. I will lop off these branches one day ; let them drag me to a law court if they like. I am ready to spend my entire fortune on the lawyers."

" Why ? " Savitri ventured. " These branches give very good shade here."

" Do you like the shade ? "

" Yes, very much."

" Very well then," said the old man as if Savitri's opinion decided the issue. " I am glad to hear it, but be certain to keep the ground here clean ; that is what you are getting your half measure of rice and a quarter of an anna for. Under this pile of withered leaves there may be cobras, and I don't like our devotees to be bitten to death here ; devotees are rare enough without cobras." Dry leaves on the cobbles crackled under their feet. At this corner there was a shanty created by enclosing the angles of the high wall with corrugated iron sheets and wooden boards. It had a rickety door. The old man unlocked it, saying, " You have no home, I believe."

" If she had a home here you would never have seen her," Ponni said.

179

"You can live in this if you like," the old man said. "Come in and have a look. It is not bad." Savitri stooped into it. It was very dark, light and air being admitted only by the chinks in the joints of the iron sheets. Rats jumped about, startled, and there was some flapping of wings above, which might be bats or sparrows. In a corner there was a gilded pedestal for carrying the image of God in procession, two or three empty kerosene tins, and some gunny-sacks. There was a blackened mud oven in another corner. Savitri withdrew her head and breathed again. "You can cook your food there, and shut yourself in when you have no work," said the old man. "But bear in mind that it is a special concession, and don't imagine that you can demand it as a right. All that you can demand is your half measure of rice and a quarter of an anna, and not this."

"Are you giving it to me as a charity?"

"Absolutely. What doubt is there? If you have any doubt ask anyone if anyone was ever given that room."

Savitri said, "I will do without the room. I will manage somehow."

"How will you manage? Do you think I will leave the shrine open and that you can go and live there? I would never do that."

"I never thought so, but I will manage.

This corridor will be home enough for me."

" Here ? " the old man exclaimed, looking up. " With the wind and sun and rain, not to mention any scoundrel who might think of jumping over the wall . . . No, no. It won't do. The temple has a name to maintain. I won't have you here if you refuse to have this room ; but don't demand it as a right."

Ponni said, " If you don't like this, come to my house when you have no work to do here."

Charity ! Charity ! Savitri was appalled by the amount of it that threatened one. "All right, I will live in this," she said, choosing the lesser charity.

The old man opened a back door and took them into the garden. A few plants, nerium, jasmine, and one or two nondescripts, grew there. There was a mud-walled well in the middle of the garden.

" I was told that you knew something of gardening. I should like you to prove it," said the old man. " Here is the water, any amount of it."

Ponni protested : " What do you mean by it, sir? You want her to do the work of four persons. You want her to do this and that endlessly in the temple ; all right, we won't grumble about it. But what is this ? This is not the temple."

" This is also a part of the temple. God must have His flowers every day."

" I know all that, but you can engage someone else to do the gardening ; we won't do it."

" Very well," said the old man. " She need not do it ; she needn't do anything."

" What do you take her for ? What do you think she is ? "

" Whatever she is, we are not concerned with it now ; she may be a king's wife or a judge's cousin. What do I care ? I am a servant of Subramanya, and I don't care for anyone in this world."

Finally Savitri intervened and said that she considered tending the garden the most agreeable part of the work. The old man spent nearly an hour in the garden. He stooped over every plant, and had a comment to make on every leaf.

When they came back to the portals he saw Mari squatting on the ground and asked, " Fellow, why are you moping here ? "

" I am waiting to prostrate myself before the god."

" I am not opening the shrine now. Come in the evening. Don't imagine that I am at the beck and call of every guttersnipe in the place. Come in the evening."

When they were about to start out Ponni

asked, " What are you doing for food today ? "

" No need to think of it now. Time enough for it. I am getting my half measure of rice."

" You will get it tomorrow," Ponni said. " Do you tell me that you are going to starve till tomorrow ? You have starved enough, I think."

" Why should anybody starve ? " the old man asked. " Come to my house. I will give you food." Savitri declined the offer. Ponni suggested to the old man that he might give a measure of rice in advance. The old man revolved it in his mind and agreed. He added, " But the quarter of an anna, she will get it only tomorrow. On no account will I give the money in advance."

" What can she do, sir, with bare rice ? She has to buy a little salt and something else to go with the rice."

The old man covered his ears with his hands. " Don't talk. I am listening to too much talk. I won't, simply won't, give the money in advance, that is all. Don't stand there and talk till my ears ache."

Ponni said, " But, sir, my master, will you give her a little firewood and a small vessel ? "

" All right. I never say ' No ' to a reasonable request." Savitri was annoyed at the number of petty details that living demanded. Ponni was overjoyed. " I will procure you a little butter-milk and salt."

" No," said Savitri emphatically. " If you bring anything I will throw it into the well."

" How are you going to eat plain rice ? "

" I can do it. If I have to take buttermilk and salt from you, why should I work for the rice alone ? You could give me that too ! "

§

Before midday Savitri had swept the corridor clean not only of the dry leaves thrown down by the mango branches but also of all the coco-nut shells and faded flowers dropped there by devotees. She dug the plants and watered them. She felt a great thrill when she lighted the oven and cooked a little rice for herself. " This is my own rice, my very own ; and I am not obliged to anyone for this. This is nobody's charity to me." She felt triumphant, and a great peace descended on her as she drank a little water, came out of the kitchen, and lay down in the shade of the mango tree. She lay with her head on the threshold of the shanty, gazing at the blue sky and at the deep green of the mango foliage. Her satisfaction at having eaten food of her own was slightly spoilt by the memory of the concessions she had to accept. She soothed her mind by telling it that she would for-go a portion of her wage for some days to compensate for the vessel and the firewood. From tomorrow she would go out and gather faggots. . . .

She felt happy to recollect the firmness with which she had declined Ponni's numerous offers. . . .

It had been rather hard to swallow bare rice, cooked in water, without adding even salt, but it was worth it because it enhanced one's sense of victory.

The cool air, the mango shade, and the noonday glare induced a drowse. She fell asleep. The sound of a bamboo staff tapping the cobbles awoke her. " Hey, get up, get up," the old man cried. Savitri opened her eyes and sat up.

" It is four o'clock and you are still sleep-ing ! "

Savitri got up and noticed that the sun had gone down the other side of the mango tree and was throwing a beam of light on the wall of the shrine.

" You think you are employed to sleep ? " asked the old man, and hobbled about, peer-ing closely at the ground. " You have left the garbage of a week ; why haven't you swept this properly ? "

Savitri looked along the way he pointed. " I don't see anything," she said, determined to overcome her timidity.

" There, there," the old man said, pointing with his stick. " Don't tell me that you are blind."

" I have good sight, but I don't see anything anywhere. I have swept the whole place thoroughly."

" Have you ? I am very glad to hear it. You appear to be a person who knows what to do. I like such persons. I don't like slackers. Come with me."

He unlocked the door of the shrine. They entered the dark shrine, which smelt of burnt lamp-oil, flowers, incense, and bats. The old man lighted a couple of tall bronze lamps. He asked, " Where are the flowers ? "

" Which flowers ? "

" Which flowers ! " the old man repeated. " Flowers in the garden. Don't ask ' Which garden ? ' Have you not gathered the flowers yet ? "

Savitri went to the garden and brought a handful of flowers. The old man took the flowers and entered the inner shrine. Savitri brought together her palms and prayed to the idol : " Protect Sumati, Babu, and Kamala. Let them all eat well and grow. Please see that they are not unhappy." The old man said, " This is the first day and so I don't mind if you are a little slack, but from tomorrow I won't show the same patience. Now take a rag and clean all the lamps and fill them with fresh oil."

" Where can I find a rag ? "

" Create one, young woman. You mustn't ask me where is this and what is that. I don't care if you have to tear a piece out of your *saree*. Work should not suffer, and the good name of the temple must be maintained at any cost. What is the use of having you here if you have got to be plaguing me like this ? That blackguard and his wife and everybody comes to plead for you. I don't care for anyone here ; be pleased to know that. That woman may have the worst tongue in the village, but I am equal to it." The old man went on talking as he bent over the idol and picked up the faded flowers on it, polished its ornaments, and decorated it with fresh flowers.

At five o'clock visitors began to arrive. Rumour had gone abroad that a mysterious woman was engaged in the temple, and this brought in more visitors than was usual. Everybody looked about, stared at Savitri, nudged each other, went round the corridor, prostrated before the image, and gave the old man the offerings. So many people kept staring at her

187

that Savitri slipped out and shut herself in the shanty.

When the voices ceased, late in the evening, she came out. In the inner shrine the old man was bundling up the coconuts, fruits, and coins that he had collected. He was very pleased. " People are once again becoming godly," he said, his small face creased in a smile, and shining in the light near the idol. He threw a piece of coconut at her and said, " Take it, it is your share."

" I don't want it. My share is only a half measure of rice."

" Take the coconut also. You are a good woman, you deserve it."

" No. I never eat coconut."

The old man was about to go home. As she saw him at the door, Savitri felt suddenly desolate. She would have to be all alone in this dark temple, with the dim oil-lamp, and stars, and the massive tree looming over the wall. The old man said, " If you are afraid to remain here, you may come to my house. You can spend the night with the womenfolk in my house."

" Of what should I be afraid ? " asked Savitri. Was there no escape from fear and charity ?

" How can I say ? " said the old man.

" I am not afraid of anything," said Savitri, and added, " I am living in God's house and He will protect me."

These brave words did not sustain her long. After the old man departed she regretted she had not accepted his offer. Everything terrified her. The whole air was oppressive ; the surrounding objects assumed monstrous shapes in the solitary hour. She fled to her shanty and bolted the door. She lit a cotton wick floating on oil in a little mud pan.

As the hours advanced and the stillness grew deeper, her fears also increased. She was furious with herself at this : " What despicable creations of God are we that we can't exist without a support. I am like a bamboo pole which cannot stand without a wall to support it. . . ."

And she grew homesick. A nostalgia for children, home, and accustomed comforts seized her. Lying here on the rough floor, beside the hot flickering lamp, her soul racked with fears, she couldn't help contrasting the comfort, security, and un-loneliness of her home. When she shut the door and put out the lights, how comforting the bed felt and how well one could sleep ! Not this terrible state. . . . And then the children. What a void they created ! " I must see them ; I must see Babu, I must see Sumati, and I must see Kamala.

Oh. . . ." But what about the fiery vows, and the coming out at midnight?

The futility, the frustration, and her own inescapable weakness made her cry and sob. " A wretched fate wouldn't let me drown first time. I can't go near the water again. This is defeat. I accept it. I am no good for this fight. I am a bamboo pole. . . . Perhaps Sumati and Kamala have not had their hair combed for ages now. . . ."

§

In the morning Savitri went over to the old man's house and told him, " I am leaving."

" What has happened ? "

" I can't keep away from my children and home."

" All right. I never asked you to come and work."

" Here is the vessel I borrowed yesterday, here is the key of the room."

" Are the things in it safe ? "

" Yes. As you see, I am carrying nothing with me."

" Hm ! There is nothing there worth taking."

They were silent for some time and he asked, " Why are you standing there ? I gave you your yesterday's wage in advance."

" Yes," she said, though he had given only the rice and not the money. " I am only waiting to take leave of you."

" All right, you can go. God's blessings be on you. Don't leave your children and wander about hereafter."

She hesitated before Ponni's house for a moment. Her first impulse was to go away without telling her. A defeat needed no proclamation. . . .

She knocked on the door. Ponni invited her in. " No. I am going. I have just come to tell you I am going home."

Ponni was overjoyed to hear it.

" At first I thought of going away without telling you."

" Ah, how could you ? "

" No, I couldn't. I will remember all my life your affection and help. God will reward you for your goodness. May He bless you with a child soon ! "

" How are you going to reach the town ? "

" Only two or three miles. I will manage ; don't worry yourself."

" Oh no, impossible," said Ponni, and came out. She shouted to her neighbour : " Sister, please keep an eye on this house. There is nobody in."

They walked down the tree-flanked highway.

Ponni explained her husband's absence. " A cart broke down somewhere and people came and pulled the poor man right out of bed, even before dawn. Poor man, he really does work hard." She stopped every passing bullock-cart to ask, " Are you going townward ? Will you take a passenger ? " At last they found a cart-man willing to take in a passenger. Ponni disputed with heat the fare the cartman demanded. It took nearly half an hour for a settlement to be reached.

" Now get into the cart, I will walk back home," Ponni said. " Go with a cheerful face. Don't look so sad. Remember : men are good creatures, but you must never give way to them. Be firm and they will behave."

" All right," Savitri said. " I will remember it." She was about to ask Ponni and her husband to visit her at South Extension, but checked herself. " Who am I to invite a guest ? "

" Murugan's blessings on you. He will protect you and your children. Mari occasionally comes to the town to earn an extra anna. I will ask him to see you," said Ponni. She wiped her eyes and stood in the middle of the road, watching, till the cart was out of sight.

Chapter Eleven

THE children sat round under the hall bulb.

Babu said, " I don't like the look of things. We must do something. I don't believe Father."

Kamala said, " Father has told us that she has gone to see grandfather."

" I don't believe it, because if she has . . . You are still children. You may believe what he says, but I don't. Don't ask why." At this Kamala showed signs of bursting into tears. Sumati put her arms around her and frowned at Babu. " Why do you frighten the child by talking in this mysterious manner ? "

Babu said, " I was only joking. Don't cry. Mother has gone to see Grandpa, she will be back soon. Don't cry, little one. I will take you to Chandru's house tomorrow and show you the electric tram he has made."

Kamala lifted her tear-filled eyes to him and asked, " Is it a promise ? "

" Yes."

" Will you swear that you won't break it ? "

" I never swear. If you don't believe me, don't believe me, that is all."

" If you do, I will cry," said Kamala, and showed signs of fulfilling the threat. Babu said, " You mustn't cry. If you do, you will never be able to read your lessons, pass your exams, and become a doctor."

" I don't want to be a doctor," said Kamala petulantly.

" What else do you want to be ? You said that when you were grown-up you wished to be a doctor like our lady doctor."

" What do you care what I am going to be ? It is none of your business."

" Don't be impertinent. Learn to behave before your elders," Babu said hotly, at which Kamala threatened to break down once again.

Sumati said, " Now, will you leave us alone or not ? I will call the cook." She called the cook and told him, " Babu is teasing me and Kamala, and won't leave us alone."

The cook held up a finger and warned Babu : " I will tell Father as soon as he comes home. Leave them alone, and go and read your books."

" Mind your own business. Who are you to command me ? "

The cook sat down on the carpet cross-legged and said, " Look me in the eyes and say it." He looked fixedly at Babu. Babu said, " All right, I will. I am not afraid of your powers of magic." The girls screamed and covered Babu's eyes with their hands, and also his mouth, in order to stop it from uttering further blasphemies.

" Take away your hands," the cook said, looking wild.

" No, no. Forgive him for our sake. He won't say such things again. Please take your eyes off him." The belief was that a person who looked into the cook's eyes at certain moments would be turned to stone. They had been told that many of the furlong and mile stones in the place were once human beings who had dared to look into the cook's eyes ; after they became stones the Government people came along, chiselled them into shape, and carved miles and furlongs on them.

The girls very nearly threw Babu down and held him away from the cook's visual range. Babu was gasping for breath. Ranga came in from somewhere at the moment, and the cook appealed to him to decide whether Babu was to be petrified or not. Ranga, after a moment's thought, said, " Leave him alone. He is more or less motherless now." He then passed on to scandal : " What is this that people are saying ? I thought things looked rather queer. . . ." He related how a friend of his working in the Engineer's house overheard the Engineer's wife saying that a certain lady's departure seemed to be rather abrupt, and as far as she knew (she also belonged to Talapur and received letters from there) there was nothing the matter with the old man ; and then Ranga's friend had heard something about a new person in the office and complications at home.

The cook said, " It may be true or it may not be. Why do you waste your time listening to gossip ? Our business is to do our business. We don't care what happens to anybody. There was some talk about it this evening at the coffee-house, and I said that the departure was rather abrupt and as far as we knew there was neither letter nor telegram about the old man's health, and if that is so how could anyone be compelled to believe the story ? It is no use compelling people to believe this or that, and I told them the truth, namely, that So-and-so has not been coming home punctually of late. Was there anything wrong in what I said ? "

" No, none," said Ranga. " You spoke only the truth, didn't you ? "

Kamala asked, " Are you talking about Mother ? "

" Why ? "

" Because if it is about Mother we want to know what you are saying."

" No. It is about someone else," the cook said. " Why should we talk about your mother ?

You were talking about someone else, weren't you, Ranga?"

"Yes, yes."

"It was about my uncle in the town who has a lot of money but is not coming home when he should, and so people want to shut him out of the house."

"Where does he go?"

"He has a number of concubines, and he stays with them."

"What are concubines?" Kamala asked.

Babu warned Ranga: "You are uttering bad words before the children. Take care."

"What is bad about the word? Don't we say ' wife '? It is a similar word."

"Why don't you drop it if it is a bad word?" Sumati asked. Kamala said, "We don't want to hear any bad word now, so leave it alone. Go on, tell me: if it was about your uncle and not about Mother you were speaking, why did you mention Grandpa in Talapur?"

"My uncle's sister's grandfather is also in Talapur and she went to see him because he was unwell."

"But you said that no letter or telegram arrived."

"Yes. No letter or telegram arrived, yet she went off rather abruptly thinking that grandfather was ill. . . . I will tell you more about it

197

while you eat. Come in for dinner. It is getting late."

Father came home. He passed straight through to the kitchen, stood on the threshold, and watched the children eat.

" How many runs did you make this evening, Babu ? "

" I got only one chance to bat, and I made twenty runs."

" Is that all ? When I was your age I never made anything under fifty. It was because I ate well and was strong. You are puny and won't eat. Look at the rice on your plate ! It is a quarter of what I used to eat at your age. Eat well, young man, and you will be able to score more runs. Here, bring some more rice for this boy."

Father looked at Kamala and said : " Why is your hair so rumpled ? Did you comb and braid it this evening ? "

" I forgot to do it, Father," said Kamala.

Sumati said, " She gave such a lot of trouble that I couldn't do it. Every day Mother had such a lot of trouble. . . ."

Ramani looked at Kamala reprovingly and said, " Is this how you conduct yourself ? Your hair is standing on end and you look like a sick person. You must be a good girl now. Sumati, you must attend to her properly. This won't do." He watched them till they finished their dinner and then went in to change.

After they had washed their hands Babu managed to take Sumati aside, and said, " Do you know what Janamma told me this evening ? "

" No."

" That Mother has not gone to Talapur. I suspected that there was some such thing."

" Where is she ? "

" Who can say ? She might have been carried away by robbers or eaten by lions or tigers."

Sumati trembled, and put her hands to her eyes. Babu sternly told her, " None of that. Don't create a scene. If you cry I will never speak to you again."

" What are we to do about it now ? " Sumati asked.

" You leave it to me. I will speak to Father and ask him to search."

" He may get angry with you."

" If he gets angry I will do something else." He had already made up his mind, as a last measure, to inform the police through his friend Chandru.

Babu waited till Kamala went to bed, and tiptoed to his father's room. He stood at the doorway and peeped in. Father was on his rattan lounge with a novel in his hand. Babu could see only Father's back and so was unable to foresee how he would be received. He wished he could get a view of his face, and tiptoed away back to his desk. Though he opened his geography and looked at it, he could not follow a single line. He felt restless. He felt that while he was sniffing at his cursed geography, his mother might be losing the last chance of being saved. He threw down the book and went once again to his father's room. He hesitated for a moment, looking at the back of Father's head. . . . Suppose Father started beating him the moment Mother was mentioned? If he did, Babu would wrench away, run out of the house, and tell Chandru to tell the police. . . . But why not wait a little while and try to catch Father some other time? He smothered this suggestion and resolutely walked in and stood before his father.

"Finished your studies for the night?" asked Father, looking over his book.

"Yes."

"Then go and sleep."

"All right, Father. But I have come to talk about Mother."

"What about her?"

"Is she alive?" And saying this he burst into tears. Ramani was slightly frightened. He himself had not been quite easy in mind since the morning. It was three days since she had left, and still there was no sign of her. While the Strong Man in him said that she couldn't have gone far and that she was bound to return when she regained sense, the Weak Man, so long unnoticed by himself, constantly pricked him with the reminder that she had been gone two days and three nights now ; and suppose she had done something very rash and foolish or something had happened to her, how was he to answer the children, her people, and everybody ? People would talk : " The wife of the Secretary of the Engladia Insurance Company . . . He shuddered. If anything happened he would have to pack out of Malgudi. . . . And now this boy.

"Why do you cry ? " he asked. Babu sobbed that he had learnt that Mother had not gone to Talapur and he had known that she hadn't gone there. Ramani felt angry. This little boy to come and cause a disturbance with his wild imaginings. "Look here, I don't like this sort of thing. Don't listen to stupid lies. Go and sleep." The boy stood still, showed no signs of moving, and his sobbing increased. Ramani looked at him in helpless anger. He felt like slapping him ; he would have done it if Savitri had been there. Now he couldn't do it.

The boy seemed to have inherited something of his mother's hysteria. He might create a very noisy scene with the other children joining in. He took Babu's hand, drew him nearer, and said, " Don't cry. Your mother is safe. You are a big boy ; you play cricket and all that ; how can you cry like a baby if your mother is absent for a little while ? "

" It is not that. It is because I suspect things," Babu said, blowing his nose, considerably mollified by his father's manner. He told his father what he had heard from Janamma. Ramani felt very uncomfortable ; he was frightened of the boy ; he couldn't stay in his company any longer. He rose from his lounge and said, " I never knew that you would feel so unhappy. I will go to the post office and send a telegram asking your mother to return at once."

" Is she really there ? "

" Of course. Why do you doubt it ? " He dressed hurriedly and started out. " I have some other business too. I may return late. If you are all afraid to be alone, you can ask the cook to sleep in the hall."

Babu announced to his sisters, " Father will be late, and he says the cook may sleep in the hall." Kamala threw up her pillow for joy. Sumati ran in to inform the cook. Babu followed her and whispered, " Father has gone to send a telegram to Mother. She will be here very soon. Father wasn't angry with me at all."

§

Ramani drove about the streets aimlessly, wondering what steps he should take now. After some time it occurred to him that he might see his friend Naidu, the Police Inspector, and talk things over with him. He might be able to help. He drove the car to the Inspector's quarters behind the Central Police Station in Market Road.

" Hallo, Ramani ! " the Inspector said. " What a rare bird you are nowadays ! What brings you here, theft, larceny, or arson ? What can I do for you ? "

" I just passed this way and thought I might as well drop in," said Ramani. He stayed with the Inspector for half an hour exchanging town gossip, and left.

He drove the car down Market Road and North Street, and reached the river. " Why have I come here ? " he asked himself. " How does one search for a lost wife ? " He sat in the car, peering across the sands into the darkness as if expecting his wife to rise from the water and come to the car. He stayed for a long time thus.

He hated himself for worrying about things. He hated Savitri for bringing him to this pass, and he hated Babu for disturbing his peace. "Everything is a bother, no peace of mind in this life." He brooded and speculated and then said, "I will wait for a day longer." He felt relieved at having found a way out of the present difficulty, however vague the exit might be. He reversed the car and retraced his way. His heart was lighter now as he drove up the silent Market Road. At the crossing he turned to his left, drove into Race-Course Road, and stopped before his office.

Chapter Twelve

IT was over an hour since she had arrived. The children's excitement had subsided. She ventured to ask, " Where is your father ? "

" Last night he went out to send the telegram and he hasn't yet come home. He said that the cook might sleep in the hall. What a fine story the cook told us ! He went on till midnight, but Babu wouldn't let him continue. . . ."

" Why did you interrupt the story, Babu ? "

" What nonsense, Mother ! Were we to keep awake all night ? "

" You could have gone away from us and slept somewhere ; you needn't have disturbed us."

" Mother, he has promised to continue the story tonight. We weren't in the least afraid at being without you. We kept the light on all night."

" Father took us all to a cinema and bought us such a lot of sweets."

The car sounded its horn outside. Kamala and Sumati ran to the gate to announce, " Mother has come ! "

" Has she ? " Ramani asked, and went into

the house. He hesitated for a fraction of a second on the doormat and then passed on to his room. Savitri sat in the passage of the dining-room, trembling. What would he do now? Would he come and turn her out of the house?

An hour later Ramani came towards her. She started up. He threw a brief look at her, noted her ragged appearance, and went into the dining-room. He said to the cook, " Hurry up, I have to be at the office. . . ." Savitri stood in the passage for some time. He had started eating. She stepped into the dining-room and stood before him, watching his leaf. She noticed a space in a corner of the leaf.

" Shall I call for some more beans ? "

" No," Ramani said without looking up.

" Curd ? " Savitri asked.

" Yes." Savitri went to the cupboard and took hold of the curd vessel.

At eight-thirty in the evening the children had finished their dinner and were sitting round Savitri, ceaselessly talking, asking questions, and quarrelling. The hooting of the car a furlong off was heard—the long blast and the slight tremolo, which Savitri's accustomed ears picked up and interpreted, " He is coming home in a sweet mood." Her habit roused her. She was about to shout to Ranga to run to the garage, fretting and fussing so that the lord's homecoming might be smooth and without annoyance. . . . She checked herself.

" The car has come," the children said, jumping up.

" What if it has ? " Savitri asked, as the car hooted continuously in front of the garage door.

" As usual Ranga is away somewhere, and the garage door is unopened," Babu said.

" Find Ranga, or go and open the door yourself," said Savitri.

Ramani paused on the doormat and threw a genial look around. " How are we all today ? " he asked, and the children made some indistinct sounds in reply. " What does your mother say ? " he asked, and the children giggled. He went in to change.

Later he asked, " Children finished their dinner ? "

" Yes," said Savitri.

" Haven't you finished yours ? "

" No."

" Waiting for me ? "

" Yes."

" What a dutiful wife you are ! " he remarked, and laughed. He was granting her the privilege to laugh and joke and be happy.

" Oh, I should have bought some jasmine for you," he said, looking at her mischievously. She tried to smile.

He watched her for a moment while she was eating. " Oh, how poorly you eat ! " he exclaimed. " Have a little more ghee. Eat well, my girl, and grow fat. Don't fear that you will make me a bankrupt by eating."

She attempted to laugh, and muttered through it, " If I grow too fat, people may not recognise me." She knew it was a miserable joke. " A part of me is dead," she reflected.

He said, " I came home early entirely for your sake, and now you won't talk to me properly. What is the matter with you ? "

" I don't know. I am all right. I am tired and want to sleep."

He pleaded with her, later : " Just a pretty half an hour. You can go to bed at ten-thirty. Just a little talk. I came home early for your sake."

" I can't even stand. I am very tired. I must sleep."

" Please yourself," he said, and went away to his room.

§

Days later, one afternoon she was lying on her carpet in the hall, half asleep. (The bench was still away at the office.) Her husband had gone to the office, the children had gone to school, the cook on his afternoon rounds, and

Ranga was in the back-yard washing clothes.

From somewhere came a voice crying, " Locks repaired, sirs, umbrellas repaired ! " Savitri rose from the carpet and sat on the sill of the window facing the street. The voice came nearer, and then she saw Mari passing in the dusty street, with his tool-bag slung over his shoulder and a couple of dilapidated umbrellas under his arm ; his dark face was shining with sweat under the hot sun.

Savitri felt excited. She could give him food, water, and a magnificent gift, and inquire about her great friend Ponni ; perhaps Ponni had sent him along now. Savitri almost called him through the window, but suddenly checked herself and let him pass. He had now passed the house. She felt unhappy at letting him go ; she felt that it was very mean and unjust. . . .

" Locks repaired, sirs ! . . ." came from the next street.

The poor fellow's face shone with sweat ; perhaps he had been tramping the streets in the hot sun, foodless ; perhaps he had not earned a pie yet in the town. How this man and Ponni had begged her to take the coconut and plantain. . . .

" Very unjust to let him go, but what can I do ? " she reflected.

She called Ranga and told him, " Call that

lock-repairer who was crying in the street just now. He must be in the next street."

" Yes, madam."

As Ranga was about to step out she changed her mind : " Let him go, don't call him." She thought : " Why should I call him here ? What have I ? "

" Locks repaired, sirs, umbrellas repaired ! " came from four or five streets off.

She sat by the window, haunted by his shining hungry face long after he was gone, and by his " Locks repaired ! . . ." long after his cry had faded out in the distance.